Raphael's Story

The true tale of an abandoned kitten
who found a forever home

by Deborah L. Courville

THE SAMOTHRACE PRESS

This is not a work of fiction. This is the true story of one kitten's journey from homelessness to happiness, insofar as it is known. Names, places, events, motives, characters, personalities and descriptions in this book are largely real, although where details are not complete, the author has used deduction and imagination to fill in the blanks. Any other interpretation is beyond the intention of the author.

For all homeless animals everywhere,
For Raphael, with love,
And for NikePurrfektCat, always

About the Author

The author of 'Raphael's Story,' Deborah L. Courville, is best known for her historical fact-based fiction. This is the first (and probably only) time she has ever written a biography, much less a biography of a cat.

Courville was inspired to write this book to call attention to several issues related to animal well being in the modern world, such as the plight of feral cats, overpopulation, declawing, cruelty and abandonment. The stories of most of the animals in this book are true.

Inspired by the difficult journey of her own cat, Raphael, the author has crafted a complete tale based on the sketchy facts of her cat's life before he came to her.

Under the *nom de plume* of Eugénie D. West, the author also writes murder mysteries that are highly acclaimed worldwide.

Find the author on Twitter at @LadyCourville and on Facebook as Deborah L. Courville.
Email:debcourville@gmail.com
Raphael (the cat) is on Twitter at @RaphaelGingrBoy

A portion of the sales of this book will be donated to the actual Rescue where the real Raphael came from, and where the author can sometimes be found cleaning litter pans and giving out treats.

Cover photo: Deborah L. Courville
End page photo: Dana B. Grubb

Raphael's Story

Chapter One

"He don't mee-ow, he squeaks!" the man told his little girl disparagingly. A smoking cigarette dangled from the man's bottom lip as he picked the small orange kitten up roughly by the scruff of his neck and tossed him around in his large, calloused hands.

"But Daddy, he's cute!" protested the little girl. She watched her father with anxious eyes. "Don't hurt him," she whispered. But her father didn't hear.

Perhaps that was all to the good.

"You can have t'other one, too, they're the last ones left," the older woman said, holding out a small black and white kitten.

The man shook his head. "Aaaaah, I dunno," he grumbled. "Twice's expensive to feed."

The older woman laughed, the wrinkles on her pasty face forming themselves into deep folds, and then relaxing as the laugh ended on a wheezy cough. "They don't eat much, and besides, you keep 'em kinda hungry, they'll catch any mice around for ya," she offered in a hopeful tone.

"Oh, please, Daddy?" the little girl intervened. As she moved, her straight brown hair, plaited into two braids, swished the faded t-shirt that covered her shoulder blades. "They'll be company for each other," she added, sweetly urging him to say 'yes' to the second kitten. It was her tenth birthday, and her father had said that she could have a kitten to mark the occasion.

"*Company?*" the little orange tabby kitten thought to himself. He was just eight weeks old, but had learned the language of the two leggeds very quickly, for he was brighter than most.

He looked over at the black and white kitten, his litter mate, who looked back at him curiously. The little orange kitten sighed. Well, he supposed the black and white could be company, of sorts. They were litter mates, but with completely different temperaments. Where the orange kitten was curious and spunky, the black and white was quiet and a bit dim—at least, that's what the orange kitten thought.

The man nodded, and the girl squealed with happiness, and took both kittens carefully in her arms.

"Mew," said the black and white kitten.

"Oh, I'll call you Moo," the little girl cooed, gazing lovingly into the small cat's green eyes. Then she turned to the little orange kitten. "And you'll be Squeaker!" she giggled delightedly. She shot a questioning gaze at her father, to see if he had heard.

He hadn't been paying attention to his daughter, but he saw her look, and so gave her a grudging smile.

The little orange kitten made an outraged grumble: what kind of names were those for cats, he wondered. 'Moo' was for a cow, maybe, and 'Squeaker' well, that had no dignity at all, it was just plain silly.

Still, he supposed the little girl would be nice to them: he could hear her heart beating as she held him and his litter mate close to her worn cotton t shirt. She was smiling in that way the two leggeds had, showing her teeth. At first, this had frightened him because to a cat, such a posture was aggressive. But his mother, a grey tabby who was old and wise beyond her five years from countless partners and litters, had explained that this bizarre looking expression meant that the two legged was pleased or happy.

The older woman, whose hand printed cardboard sign at the end of the driveway reading 'free kittens' had brought the man and his daughter to her, sighed now. That was the last of them. The mother cat, whom she called Mary, would be coming with her when she moved the following week. She had finally decided to leave the chill of northeastern Pennsylvania for the sunny climes of Florida, and her old mini van was already packed with everything she would take to her new home. There wasn't much left: the kittens had been the last of her responsibilities.

She'd have to see about getting Mary spayed, since she was going to be in an apartment, not a house, and the cat would be indoors.

She handed the man a cardboard box with only three flaps. "Here, put 'em in this 'till you get 'em home," she advised with a nod to the kittens.

The man held the box open while his daughter, whose name was Jenna, carefully deposited her furry burden inside. Then they quickly shut the top.

"*Hey, hold on!*" Squeaker protested as his paw pads hit the cardboard base of the box and the top closed, engulfing him and Moo in near darkness. "*What are you doing? What's going on? Where's mom?*" he cried out.

Moo joined in with a few faint calls of, "*Mother! Mom???*"

Squeaker felt movement, then a thump, and then he heard an engine start up. It was warm and shady inside the box, for it was mid September, and the vibrations lulled the kittens nearly to sleep. Then the vibrations, and the engine, stopped, and the little girl got out of the car, carrying the box of kittens with her.

Squeaker and Moo had arrived at their new home.

Chapter Two

"*I'm hungry,*" whispered Moo. He, like his brother, had learned very fast that if they made too much noise, Jenna's father would give them a hearty smack to shut them up. One of Moo's baby teeth had been loosened this way, and had already fallen out.

Squeaker had been slapped into a wall once when the man was 'disciplining' the kittens, and his leg had fractured. It hurt, now, when he walked, but he tried very hard not to cry out, fearful of what the man might do yet again.

"*I know, so am I,*" Squeaker replied. It was evening. Jenna had come home from school and done her homework. The kittens, who kept largely to the little girl's bedroom, had ventured out from beneath her bed where they had spent the day, and had played together while Jenna studied.

Then it had been dinner time—for the two leggeds, not for the kittens. It hadn't smelled especially appetizing, but since Squeaker and Moo had only had a few bits of kibble each that morning, almost anything edible was enticing.

But no table scraps had been forthcoming, and the two kittens had retired with Jenna to her room when she'd gone to bed. Now, they were huddled together in the same box they'd been transported in several weeks before; an old towel had been placed in the bottom, and the sides had been cut down so the box was open. The kittens would have much preferred curling up next to the little girl for the night, but her father disapproved of that. So Jenna had made their bed for them, and she seemed pleased when they used it. So they did.

Now, the house was dark, and relatively quiet, although the sound of a television playing somewhere a couple of rooms away was distantly audible. The single window in Jenna's room was closed, as the evenings were turning cool, but both kittens could feel a draft of air from a crack where the frame did not fit snugly.

"*I know there are mice in the walls,*" Squeaker murmured. "*I hear them.*"

"*So do I,*" Moo agreed eagerly. "*But—we can't get inside the walls,*" he finished sadly.

Squeaker frowned. When he did this, the fur between his eyes drew close in furrows of orange and white stripes, and his eyes—which were the clear, yellow-green of Chartreuse liqueur had he but known, —narrowed.

"*These are pretty flimsy walls,*" he replied knowingly. "*Not like the ones at the farmhouse,*" he added, referring to their birthplace.

"*Well, this isn't a farmhouse. It's an old house that's been knocked into apartments,*" Moo said.

"*Exactly!*" Squeaker agreed. "*And I think these walls are, well, I'm not sure what they're made of but they're not impenetrable,*" he declared stoutly.

"*They're not what?*" Moo questioned.

"*It's a word I heard Jenna say when she was learning her vocabulary,*" Squeaker replied. "*It means you can't get through it,*" he explained.

"*Oh.*" Moo paused. "*I don't know why you do it,*" he grumbled.

"*Do what?*"

"*Learn the language of the two leggeds,*" Moo replied grumpily. "*Where do you think knowing fancy words like that is going to get you? Mother taught us the basics. That's enough.*"

Squeaker tipped his head to one side and regarded his litter mate. "*I guess, I'm hoping someday one of the two leggeds will realize I can understand almost everything they say, and actually speak to me,*" he replied, a little sad.

"*But they do speak to us, all the time!*" declared Moo.

"*No, no I mean really talk to us. A—a con-ver-sa-tion!*" he pronounced, recalling another vocabulary word. "*Not just, 'good kitty' and 'no' and stuff like that,*" he told Moo.

"*Why?*" asked Moo. "*D'you think it would make them any nicer to us?*" he asked glumly.

Squeaker tipped his head to the other side. "*I don't know. Maybe. Maybe if they realized we have feelings, and hopes and dreams and fears and worries, just like they do, they would be nicer to us,*" he whispered.

Moo snorted. He was about three minutes older than Squeaker and often felt this meant he was wiser. However, he was usually incorrect.

"*Anyway, the mice in the walls,*" Squeaker continued, getting back on topic. "*Follow me,*" he whispered, and cautiously put one paw, then another, outside the box until his pads were on the scuffed linoleum floor of Jenna's room.

"*Where are we going?*" Moo whispered.

"To get dinner," Squeaker replied, and slunk away towards a far corner of the room, belly low to the ground.

Chapter Three

"*That was pretty tasty,*" Moo admitted, licking his lips and the long white whiskers that sprouted from his muzzle. They were quite striking against the mostly black fur on his face. His lower legs were white, too, and he had a large white patch on both flanks.

"*Yes, it was,*" Squeaker agreed happily.

He had led Moo to a corner of Jenna's room where the vinyl wainscoting had come unglued. The wainscoting had been part of a recent renovation, covering stains, many layers of faded wallpaper and a few holes in the plaster walls. It was one of these holes that Squeaker, who had an adventurous spirit, had discovered during previous patrols of Jenna's room.

He had clawed cautiously at the bottom corner of the vinyl until it had lifted up by several inches. The resulting space had been big enough for the two undernourished kittens to squeeze through. They had discovered a warren of rodent tunnels, far too small for them to navigate, but smelling delightfully appetizing. So they had crouched, silent and watchful, and after a relatively short while they had been rewarded when an unsuspecting *mus musculus* had trotted along, right into their paws.

Now, the kittens were back in their box bed, their bellies full, at least for the moment.

"*We should do that again,*" Moo noted, curling up nose to tail and preparing to sleep.

"*Yes, but we can't do it too often or the mice will get wise to us,*" Squeaker agreed. His brow furrowed again. *"I wish we could get out of this room at night,"* he whispered as he made himself into a round shape next to his brother. His ginger and cream fur made him look a bit like an over-large cinnamon bun. *"I'm sure there are other spots we could infiltrate, spots where the mice travel, and we could switch around which place we go, and catch them unaware,"* Squeaker explained.

" *'Infiltrate?'* " echoed Moo. *"Another word from Jenna, right?"* his tone was sleepily sarcastic.

Squeaker sighed. Moo was all right, but he didn't understand him at all.

The weeks passed, and the weather got cold. During the old home's renovations, the space that was now Jenna's room had been walled off in such a way that only half a heat register blew warm air from the furnace's ducts into the little girl's room. Her bed was next to the vent, but her father cracked her bedroom door open, as well, on the theory that heat from the rest of the apartment would also warm his daughter's room.

This meant that, as Squeaker had hoped, the kittens were now able to creep about at night very quietly and search for other routes of entry into the walls of the hundred and fifty year old structure. They were nearly silent on their small, padded paws, and since they did not need to communicate verbally and could see well in the dark, they escaped notice.

They didn't catch mice every night, for as Squeaker had predicted, the mice were canny and learned quickly that cats would sometimes be lying in ambush in certain places.

But two or three times a week they did manage a feast, of sorts, and between that and the kibble they were doled out every morning, they stayed alive.

"Yer feedin' 'em too much," complained the man one evening to his daughter. Both kittens were sitting quietly at one side of the small kitchen table, hoping for scraps from what smelled like a fried chicken dinner. "Lookit them bellies," he insisted, pointing with a mashed potato and gravy laden fork at the two kittens.

"*We're not over fed,*" grumbled Squeaker quietly, "*we've got worms. That's why our bellies look full.*" He knew Jenna, who was responsible for cleaning their litter box in the corner behind her bedroom door, was not observant enough to discover this. He didn't blame the little girl.

"No, Daddy, honest!" Jenna exclaimed, her eyes huge as she protested. "I only give them a quarter cup each, and I use the measuring scoop!" she insisted.

The man grunted, and shoveled another mouthful of food in. "Well, better make it a quarter cup for the both of 'em," he declared. "You hear me? They start costin' me too much and they're out, Jenna."

Jenna gulped. "Ok. Daddy. Ok," she whispered.

That night before Jenna went to bed, she opened a small box she kept between her mattress and box spring at the foot of her bed. In this, she kept what she thought of as her 'treasures.' The box was no more than four inches square, and quite shallow, but Jenna did not have many treasures.

It contained a little ring her Mother had bought her for her eighth birthday, just weeks before she had died. Also in the box was a silk rose bud Jenna had found on the sidewalk in the spring—doubtless blown off from someone's outdoor decoration, but Jenna thought it was very pretty. There was also a book of poems the school library had been getting rid of along with boxes of other books, destined for third world countries. Students had been given first pick of the unwanted books before they were shipped off, and Jenna had eagerly chosen the small volume.

And finally, rolled up and stuffed in the toes of a pair of white ankle socks she'd long since outgrown, was all of Jenna's birthday money. She had been saving her birthday money since she'd received that first gift from her Grandmother when she'd been five. She had had no occasion to spend any, so Jenna had several dollars saved up.

"I'll stop at the gas station tomorrow and buy you a box of cat food," Jenna whispered to Squeaker and Moo as she tucked the meager bills safely in her school knapsack.

"*Good thing, too,*" Moo groused.

"*Thank you, Jenna,*" Squeaker said politely. "*But what we really need is to visit the vet.*"

Jenna smiled over at the orange kitten's squeaking noises. "You're welcome," she whispered as she climbed into bed.

"*She understood me!*" Squeaker exclaimed, delighted.

"*Oh, be quiet,*" Moo hissed to his brother. "*She did not. She was just answering what she pretended you said!*" he insisted. "*And if you're not happy for the extra food, I'll have your share, I'm always hungry! And I don't want to go to a vet,"* he grumbled.

"You need to, though, and so do I," murmured Squeaker worriedly as he hunkered down next to Moo in their box. The old towel in the bottom was rancid, fur covered and dirty, since it had never been washed. What fleas were not buried in Squeaker's thick orange fur or Moo's black and white coat, lived in the towel's folds. But it was something, even if it wasn't much.

Chapter Four

Jenna's scheme to buy a box of cat food worked, for a while. She could only afford the cheapest kind, but estimated that she would have enough money to buy kibble for a couple of months before her funds ran out. Each box lasted a couple of weeks, for she did not give the cats too much. She fed Moo and Squeaker when she was doing her homework and knew her father wouldn't bother her.

Jenna kept the box of cat food in the mini mart's plastic bag, knotted at the top. This was then placed in a drawer of Jenna's small dresser, under her summer t shirts and shorts. Squeaker and Moo couldn't get to it, even though Squeaker spent many otherwise dull hours while Jenna was at school staring at the dresser drawer and wondering how he could manage to open it.

Squeaker and Moo grew: by mid December they were just about six months old. They still caught mice a couple of times a week, but their size meant that the spots they could fit into inside the old house's walls were fewer, so catching mice was a more difficult task than it had been.

Although the holidays were supposed to be a jolly, happy time, Jenna's father seemed more and more morose and Jenna seemed more and more subdued. Squeaker, who paid attention to things like this, sensed that Jenna was afraid to ask her father what was wrong. The kitten had never seen the man strike his daughter as he did the cats, but he suspected that Jenna was fearful of upsetting or angering her father nonetheless.

Finally, one day when Jenna's father came home, he flung a letter down on the kitchen table and slumped in a chair. He bellowed his daughter's name and she jumped up from where she'd been doing her last homework of the semester, and ran out of her room and into the kitchen.

"Yes, Daddy?"

Squeaker padded to the door of Jenna's room which she had left ajar, and listened with all his might.

"You better start packin' yer things," her father told her.

"But—why, Daddy?"

A logical question, Squeaker thought to himself.

The man let out a long sigh and Squeaker heard sounds of movement: the man had pulled Jenna onto his knee, he thought.

"There ya go, Jenna: you're my best girl, you know that don't cha?" he asked in a sugar-coated voice.

Squeaker couldn't hear Jenna's reply.

"What are you doing?" Moo asked, appearing suddenly at Squeaker's shoulder.

"*Sssshhhh...I'm listening. Something's happening. I'm trying to hear what,*" Squeaker instructed his brother.

Moo was silent.

"Well, Jenna, we're goin' to a new place," the man said, his tone suggesting that this was the most wonderful thing in the world.

"We are? Why?" Jenna queried.

"Because—you know the plant shut down, don't you, girl?" the man asked rhetorically.

26

Squeaker thought he could hear the swish of Jenna's braids as she nodded.

"And since then I been doin' the best I can to get a new place, and meanwhile, doin' whatever odd jobs I can lay my hands on," the man continued. He recited a number of temporary jobs: his litany of failed attempts. "But 'snever enough." He sighed resignedly again. "I gotta put food on the table and clothes on our backs and shoes on our feet and I ain't had enough to make rent. Gotta keep the lights on and the heat on," he continued morosely.

Jenna reached over and took the letter her father had tossed on the table in her small fingers. Squeaker heard the paper rustle, then he heard the little girl's exclamation of dismay as she read.

"But Daddy, this says we—"

Squeaker heard the paper crumple suddenly, and then he heard the back legs of the kitchen chair scrape against the floor. Jenna's father had stood up, he surmised, and Jenna with him.

"We're goin' to my sister's," Jenna's father said in a tone of finality. "She's got a double wide, plenty of room for us there," he continued. "I already asked, and you're gonna share a room with your cousin Diane, and I'll bunk in with the boys."

Jenna knew her Aunt Sue and her husband Stu had a daughter a little older than she was and two sons who were younger than she was.

"Won't that be crowded?" Jenna ventured timidly.

"It's just temporary, baby," her father reassured her. "Your Uncle Stu's gonna get me in at the mill where he works and then we can get our own place."

He paused. "Ok? How does that sound, Jenna. All right?"

Jenna's agreement was quiet and unenthusiastic, but really, what choice did she have?

Chapter Five

The changes happened very quickly, for in truth there wasn't much to pack. All of Jenna's belongings fit inside two small battered suitcases and her school knapsack. Her father had instructed her to tell no one where they were going, or even that they were moving. So, as it was the Christmas holidays, Jenna had said goodbye to her teachers and classmates as though she'd be returning with them in January, even though she knew by then she and her father would be far away.

Aunt Sue lived in South Carolina, and they would be driving her father's beat up old Honda down, packed with all their things. Whatever did not fit, they left.

Jenna had actually been quite happy to obey her father and keep their relocation a secret. The circumstances made her ashamed: her Dad losing his job was bad enough, but they were being evicted, and that was something Jenna didn't want anyone to know.

They left very early in the morning on the day before Christmas, planning to drive straight through. Jenna's father told her that with no traffic problems and a little luck, they would be at his sister's place 'just about the time Ol' Saint Nick's droppin' off yer presents.'

Jenna no longer believed in Santa Claus: not since her Mother had died. But she somehow understood that her father in that moment at least needed for her to believe in the fantasy.

So she had smiled, and nodded, and handed him her two suitcases and knapsack.

"Be right back, Daddy," she whispered. It was still dark out, and everyone in the rest of the old house's apartments and in similar dwellings on both sides all up and down the street were still asleep.

"Where're ya goin'?" he asked quickly. "We gotta go, Jenna."

"I have to go get Squeaker and Moo, Daddy," Jenna began. "I fixed their box with tape and a piece of cardboard so they will be okay, I think..." she bit her lip. She had also cleaned and prepared the litter box, but didn't know if her Dad would allow her to bring that, as well: it was a bit smelly, after all, despite her efforts.

"Oh, no, no, no, Jenna, them cats ain't comin'" with us," Jenna's Dad whispered harshly.

Jenna just looked at him, appalled. "What?" she whispered, a hitch in her throat.

Her father looked at his daughter for a moment and despite the gloom he could see tears starting to trickle down her cheeks. He had hoped to avoid the issue, hoped, actually, that in the excitement of moving she'd forget about the two kittens. But...

"Now, look," he began, bustling Jenna back inside the house. Their apartment was on the ground floor, at the back, and the house's old back door was their front door. Convenient.

The minute they were inside the house, Jenna started: "they won't be any trouble, Daddy, they're good kitties, really..." she insisted as her father marched her into the kitchen where he grabbed the half-full bag of cat food, and then on back to her bedroom.

He opened the door. Squeaker was sitting on the chipped, dirty windowsill and Moo was lying on the foot of Jenna's box spring: the mattress had been rolled up and secured to the Honda's roof and covered with a tarp. When the door opened, both cats' heads snapped around to see what was going on.

"Look: you leave 'em the rest of the food, and their box and such, and they'll be fine," her Dad instructed, shaking the bag of food so the kibble inside rattled. His voice was confident. "The heat's set to come on at 50F so the pipes don't freeze, so they'll be warm enough with them fur coats," he declared. "And that landlord'll have this place rented in no time and then they'll have people to look after 'em again. We can't bring 'em to my sister's," he repeated. "There's no room."

"But Daddy, they can stay in my room..." Jenna began.

"You won't have your own room," he replied harshly, feeling guilty, and then angry, for being in this position and placing his daughter in the same situation. "You're sharing with your cousin, remember? And she's allergic!" he added with sudden inspiration.

He should have thought of that before. It would have fixed everything. But he'd been so concerned about moving, and doing it so the landlord couldn't find them and demand the back rent, he'd thought of little else.

He'd make it up to Jenna, he resolved silently, as he watched his daughter fill the cats' little dishes to overflowing, and then leave the bag with the remainder of the food where they could get to it.

The other box of extra food was, of course, packed carefully in her suitcase. There was no way, she knew, with her suitcase in the car now, that she could retrieve it. Not without angering her father and that was not something she ever wanted to do, but especially before a ten hour car trip!

She filled the cats' water bowl, too, making the trip back and forth to the bathroom sink in silence, except for her sniffles.

Then she knelt on the floor next to where the two kittens were eating: at the sound of the kibble they had both raced to their bowls and now both their faces were shoved into the food.

"*Wow, this is a lot of food,*" Moo noted around the kibble he was devouring.

"*I know—I wonder why?*" Squeaker pondered as he, too, ate quickly.

Jenna knelt next to them, then, and stroked their fur.

"I'm sorry," she whispered.

"*Why are you sorry?*" Squeaker asked, looking up at the little girl briefly.

"I thought we were taking you with us," Jenna went on. A few tears fell on Moo's black and white fur, but he didn't notice, as he was too busy eating.

"*Taking us with you...you're moving today!*" Squeaker said with sudden realization. He'd understood that they were moving, but had not realized the hour had come. "*Now?!*" he exclaimed.

Jenna was very upset. Squeaker had only seen her eyes leak a few times before, and usually it had been when she'd been missing her mother. But he thought he understand why she was crying now.

"*You aren't taking us when you move?*" Squeaker whispered, looking up at the little girl who had been the only two legged to ever show him real affection.

Jenna burst into silent tears and picked Squeaker up in her arms. "Daddy says we can't take you," Jenna went on. She sniffled and tried to wipe her wet cheeks with one hand while she held the kitten in the other. "He says a new family will move in here real soon, though, and they'll take care of you," she hiccuped to a disbelieving Squeaker. "I've left you all the food there is, and water, and..." here she dropped her voice even lower. Her father had left the doorway of her room, but he was still in the house and she didn't want him to hear her. "I'm sorry, I packed the other food, but there's a lot here," Jenna murmured, so low that the kittens could hardly hear her. "And I left the sink in the bathroom dripping a little, in case the water runs out."

Squeaker heard Jenna's father call, "Jenna! C'mon, we gotta go!" in an urgent stage whisper. "Now!" he added for good measure.

"Good bye, Squeaker," Jenna whispered, setting him back on the floor with a final stroke of his fur. "Good bye Moo," she said, stroking the other kitten as well.

"*Please don't leave us! I don't know what to do!*" Squeaker squealed suddenly, panicking. Jenna had said her father had told her to leave the cats, not take them along to wherever they were going. He had said that 'new people' would come, and take care of the kittens.

But Squeaker was not so sure.

Jenna stood, then, and Squeaker heard her father call to her once more.

"I have to go," Jenna whispered.

"Please don't leave us!" Squeaker pleaded again, abandoning his food dish and following after Jenna as she ran out of her room and to the front door where her father waited.

Quickly, the two leggeds slipped through the door and shut it. Squeaker heard the lock engage, and then a set of keys fell through the letter slot onto the threadbare mat.

Chapter Six

"So, they just left?" Moo asked, probably for the tenth time that day.

Squeaker sighed. *"Yes. Jenna said a new family will come soon, and they will take care of us,"* he repeated.

Moo just looked at his brother. *"You think so?"*

Squeaker tipped his head to one side. *"I hope so,"* he replied grimly.

There was quite a lot of food, certainly enough for a few days, especially if they were careful not to binge. Moo had already thrown up what he'd eaten that morning: what a waste.

But Moo wasn't well, Squeaker knew. Not that he was in robust health, but Moo seemed worse. He slept almost all of the time, and although he was hungry, the tapeworm got most of anything he ate, so his fur was dull and dry and he was thinner than he had been.

Now that they had the run of the small apartment, Squeaker had found a stack of old newspapers in a corner of the kitchen. They had been used to wrap the few pieces of crockery Jenna and her Dad had packed and taken with them. But Squeaker didn't know that, and didn't care: he just started using the newspaper pile as his own personal litter box, leaving Moo the one in Jenna's room. He also had worms, but somehow had escaped a tapeworm, though both were plagued with fleas.

Moo seemed content to sleep on the box spring. Squeaker had pulled the old towel—which Jenna had washed, so it was now quite clean—out of the cardboard box and dragged it onto the mattress, too.

Squeaker, however, enjoyed exploring the apartment at his leisure, and found several other places where he could wriggle under a loose piece of paneling or wainscot and gain entry to the house's inner walls—and mice! True, they had quite a lot of food, but not so much that a mouse or two wasn't a tasty treat. And if the new two leggeds didn't come right away, as Jenna had expected, then once the food ran out, having access to a source of rodents would be very important.

The late December weather was chilly, but when the sun was out, it streamed in the dirty windows and warmed the apartment nicely. At night, the two kittens snuggled together for warmth.

Often once it was dark, Squeaker pushed aside the limp sheet that served as a curtain in Jenna's room, so he could see directly into an apartment in the house next door. For days, he had been watching a bustle of activity over there, but the first night after Jenna and her father had left, something magical happened.

"*Moo—come here!*" called Squeaker from the window sill.

"*Why? What? I just want to sleep,*" his brother replied from the mattress.

"*No—you gotta see this!*" Squeaker insisted.

Grumbling, Moo got up slowly, stretched, scratched, and ambled over to the window where his brother was. He wasn't sure he could jump up to the window sill: he had no energy at all.

"*Come on, you can do it,*" Squeaker urged.

Moo jumped, missed, and more or less clawed his way up until he sat next to Squeaker on the sill.

"*Now—look, look over there!*" Squeaker instructed.

Moo looked through the cracked and dirty pane of glass and saw a lighted room in an apartment in the house next door. There were two leggeds inside the room, and he could see a big golden-furred dog, and a grey tabby cat in the window. But most remarkable was a tall thing in the middle of the room, with all sorts of shiny and sparkly things on it.

"*That—that looks like a tree,*" Moo offered hesitantly. He knew he wasn't as smart as his younger brother, and sensed that his statement was ridiculous. Still, that is what he saw. "*But trees grow in the forest, not in two leggeds' houses,*" he mumbled in an attempt to exonerate himself.

"*Yes, you're right,*" Squeaker agreed. "*I think that's what the two-leggeds call a 'Christmas Tree,'*" he ventured. "*I heard Jenna talking about it. They usually have one, she said, but didn't get one this year, since they were moving.*"

Moo blinked. "*Hmmm...so you knew they were moving?*" Moo asked his brother.

Squeaker nodded. "*I knew. But I thought we were going with them, since that is what Jenna seemed to think, too,*" Squeaker replied, staring at the grey tabby in the other window.

She hadn't seen them yet, but Squeaker could tell she was well fed and healthy, and her fur shone in the light from the room. She had a leather strap around her neck, too, with small round things dangling from it. He wondered what those were.

Moo was dozing, his head drooping towards his folded paws.

"*Moo—look at this!*" Squeaker urged a little while later, tapping his brother on his nose to wake him.

"*What! I almost fell off!*" Moo exclaimed crossly.

"*Sorry to startle you,*" Squeaker murmured. "*But look!*" He turned once more to the window.

In the house next door, a young woman and a few friends had gathered. They were eating things from little plates, and drinking from tall glasses, and they seemed to be admiring the tree. Then, the lights on the tree were switched on and Squeaker let out a mew of excitement when the tree exploded into brilliance.

"*Wow, look at that!*" Moo exclaimed. "*I have never seen that before.*"

"*Neither have I,*" agreed Squeaker. "*It's beautiful!*"

They both watched, mesmerized, as the young woman moved over towards the tabby in the window, and leaned down to stroke her under her chin.

"*Ooooh, I bet that feels good,*" murmured Squeaker longingly.

"*Yeah,*" noted Moo, sounding sad.

The young woman then gave the tabby several treats from a small bag in her hand, then stroked the cat again, and gave her a kiss on her head, right between her ears.

"*What were those?*" Squeaker wondered aloud.

"*Food,*" Moo replied with certainty.

"But they were in a tiny little bag," Squeaker protested. *"They must have been special Christmas food or something,"* he murmured, still watching in amazement: this seemed like some kind of wonderful dream.

Now, one of the young woman's friends was doing much the same with the golden retriever: he petted him on his head, and then gave him what looked like a huge rawhide bone. The dog grabbed the treat in his jaws and immediately started chomping away happily on it.

Squeaker's stomach rumbled. He was hungry: better go have some more kibble.

"Maybe those nice two leggeds next door will take care of us," Moo commented hopefully as Squeaker hopped down and made his way towards their food bowls.

"How would they know we are here?" Squeaker asked, somewhat sharply, for the leg he'd fractured, though largely healed, hurt tonight. That probably meant bad weather coming: he had noticed that the day before a storm the old fracture pained him.

"I don't know...hey, you're limping," Moo said, sounding concerned. *"You don't usually limp anymore. What's wrong?"*

Squeaker began eating. *"It hurts when the weather's going to get bad,"* he explained in between mouthfuls. *"It's fine. Don't worry."*

Chapter Seven

A few days passed in a similar fashion: Squeaker would explore the apartment and check what he thought of as his 'mouse holes' for any unlucky rodents who were passing by. But the kibble filled his belly and he was less motivated now that he was eating enough.

At night, he would sit in the window in Jenna's room and watch the house next door. The young woman who apparently lived there with the grey tabby cat had more visitors over—the dog had been with one of the visitors, and did not return. But others came, bearing boxes and large bags and the young woman seemed excited when the other two leggeds came to see her and the tree, and her grey tabby.

Squeaker could sense the young woman's exhilaration and happiness. He could almost taste the treats she gave to her grey tabby nearly every evening. He could practically feel the softness of the plush new cat bed he spied. The young woman had placed this on a table that abutted a window sill, and the grey tabby alternated between watching from her usual window and curling up in her new bed at the other.

Two days after Christmas, three feet of snow fell in a howling blizzard that blocked the sun and left everything looking as though it had been dipped in marshmallow creme. It didn't matter much to Squeaker and Moo: they were, at least, inside. And the snow muffled everything so that the world seemed oddly tranquil and serene.

And then, a day or so later, the door to the apartment opened, and a tall, big boned two legged stepped in, followed by two more two leggeds: a chubby young woman and a lanky young man. Squeaker heard the rattle of keys and the sound of the door, and he peeked around the door jamb of Jenna's room, to see what was going on.

"This here's the kitchen," the big boned two legged said to the young couple. "And down there's the living room..."

"*Moo! Moo wake up!*" Squeaker said excitedly, nudging his brother.

"*What? Why?*" Moo asked, as always.

"*The new two leggeds are here! They'll take care of us now. They're here, they're here!*" Squeaker nearly danced with joy on his little pink paw pads.

The arrival of the new family was certainly fortuitous, he thought. The night before, the mice who inhabited the old house had discovered the kittens' stash of food.

Although Squeaker had tried to scare the mice away, he'd been no match for all of them, and a surprising amount of food had disappeared. Squeaker knew that more mice would come now, and that their food supply would be gone very soon. He had eaten as much as he could that morning for breakfast, and urged Moo to eat, too, although his brother seemed less and less interested in food.

Now, Squeaker sat up prettily on the mattress and curled his tail around his toes. He tried to get Moo to do the same, to look proper and polite, to welcome their new family, but Moo just grumbled and curled up to sleep again.

His ears were very warm to Squeaker's touch, and his nose was runny. This morning, Squeaker had noticed that when Moo breathed, it made a rattling noise in his lungs. Squeaker knew that wasn't good. He desperately hoped their new family would bring them both to the vet, as soon as possible!

Squeaker blinked his eyes now, and adjusted his pose so he would look as handsome as he could. He glanced over at Moo. Well, he supposed a sleeping kitty was appealing, too.

"And this is the other bedroom, it's small, but it'd make a good nursery," the big boned two legged said in a suggestive tone, stepping into the room. "Well, well, well what have we here?" he asked, not unkindly.

"*Hello*," said Squeaker. "*Our two leggeds left us behind when they moved. It wasn't our fault. We are here to welcome our new family!*" he said.

"Oh, goodness, what is that smell?" shrieked the young woman who, along with the lanky young man, had also entered the room.

"Aw, it's just cats," the big boned two legged replied, clocking the overflowing, dirty litter box behind the door. "The previous tenants—I told you about them, didn't I? Just up and left and behind on three months' rent I'll never see—musta left 'em here," the big boned two legged told them.

"Ugh, they're disgusting!" the chubby young woman said, screwing up her face and wrinkling her nose.

Squeaker was offended. He wasn't disgusting, and neither was Moo. They'd been doing the best they could, all on their own! Nervously, he licked at his shoulder.

"And they're covered in fleas!" exclaimed the young man, who had stepped a little closer to see the kittens. "I'm sorry, we can't have that," he told the big boned two legged in a grave voice.

"Oh, well, I didn't know as they were here," said the big boned two legged, very fast. "Umm, I'll be, ummm...fumigating the place, and doing a little painting and such in the next couple days. And the cats'll be gone." He paused. "If you want, you could move in next week," he wheedled.

"*Gone?*" echoed Squeaker. What on earth did he mean? Maybe he meant that he was going to take them with him—whoever he was, and wherever he lived. He must be the landlord, Squeaker decided a moment later. The chubby lady and the skinny man were prospective new tenants.

And they didn't want him or Moo.

Jenna had been wrong.

"Well, see that you get rid of them!" the skinny man said brusquely, and everyone turned to go. "We'll want to see the place again before we decide, anyway. When can we do that?" he asked. Their voices faded as they all moved away, and left the apartment.

Squeaker never heard the landlord's reply, but his stomach clenched in anxiety. Would the landlord come get them? When?

The landlord came and got them, not more than twenty minutes later. Unceremoniously he grabbed Squeaker and the still-sleeping Moo, carried them out the door and deposited them in the snow. A path had been shoveled from the doorway to the driveway and then to the street. Next to the driveway were some tall hedges, and then the driveway of the house next door.

That driveway had also been shoveled, and there were paths leading to the front and back doors of that house, as well, and to its big wraparound porch.

The landlord went back inside the apartment, and a few seconds later he left, carrying a large dark green garbage bag in one hand. Squeaker could smell that in the bag were the remains of what little cat food they'd still had, as well as their litter box and the newspapers he'd been using.

The landlord spied the two kittens, still sitting where he had tossed them, in the snow.

"Go on—get lost, you're not wanted here!" he shouted, and kicked snow onto them with one booted foot.

The kittens jumped when the two legged shouted and the snow fell on them, and ran into the driveway and under the hedges where they were more or less hidden.

"Squeaker, what's going on? What happened?" Moo asked faintly, looking around him. He was crouched low, and Squeaker knew he hurt. He could hear Moo gasping as he spoke: breathing was getting harder for him.

"The landlord threw us out," Squeaker replied.

"What do you mean?"

"The new family doesn't want us. And he threw us out," Squeaker repeated.

"*But—but you throw garbage out,*" Moo *protested weakly.* "*We're not garbage!*" he finished, and then, shivering, he got quiet.

"*No. We're not garbage. But we can't stay here,*" Squeaker said firmly. "*Come on…*"

"*No, I don't want to move. I want to sleep,*" Moo protested.

"*You'll freeze to death,*" Squeaker insisted. "*We have to find shelter. Come on!*" he urged, and finally, Moo moved, slowly, following his brother out the other side of the hedges and along one of the shoveled paths.

Squeaker surveyed the house next door: maybe one of the families who lived here would take them in? Maybe that lovely young woman with the grey tabby? She already had a cat, perhaps she would like a couple more? But right now, they had to find somewhere to curl up for the night where they'd be safe and, well, as warm as possible.

His sharp eyes spotted an irregularity in the latticework that skirted the porch. Almost pushing Moo, Squeaker made his way through the snow to the side of the house where the stone foundation met the edge of the porch: the lattice that extended from the porch edge to the ground was not fastened too securely, and he and Moo could just squeeze through.

Under the porch, it was at least dry, although it wasn't very warm. The sun didn't quite reach beneath the porch's edge. But up against the house's foundation a small crack leaked warm air whenever the furnace turned on.

All manner of odd detritus littered the space under the porch. Squeaker dragged a piece of cardboard over next to the foundation and urged Moo onto it. They had no towel or blanket, but the cardboard was dry and they were sheltered. Squeaker could smell mice, too, and knew that with a little luck, he'd be able to catch enough to at least keep him and Moo alive.

He shot a worried glance over at his brother. Poor Moo. Squeaker knew he was very ill, and thought that he'd given up hope. He sighed. Perhaps Moo was right. No one wanted them. Their family had abandoned them. The new family called them 'disgusting.' Even the landlord hadn't at least taken them to a shelter, he'd just tossed them out and told them to scram.

Squeaker was possessed, like most ginger tabbies, of an optimistic, good natured personality. He had endured their less than perfect treatment by Jenna and her father—well, it wasn't Jenna's fault, she'd tried—trying to be grateful that he and Moo had a home and trying to find joy in small things. He had weathered each adversity with pluck and spirit, and hadn't complained.

But as dark crept in this night, and the temperature dropped further still, and he watched his brother's labored breathing, Squeaker felt hope drain away.

Chapter Eight

"Well, hello! Who are you?" asked the young woman. It was a few weeks later. The snow had melted and compacted and most walkways and driveways were bare now, though piles and drifts of dirty grey coldness still stood in gardens and corners.

The woman, a nurse who worked the twelve-hour overnight shift at a nearby hospital, was just returning home. The early February sun had started to climb higher in the sky, and although the air was still very cold, the sun was a bit warmer each day.

This had cheered Squeaker, for now he was on his own: Moo had died less than a week after they had taken refuge under the porch of the house next door.

He'd gone quietly, with Squeaker cuddled close to him, and once he knew his brother's spirit had gone, Squeaker had done his best to dig a little depression in the loose dirt under the porch, and place Moo's small body in it. He'd covered it well, dragging whatever rubbish that was around over to the place to make a relatively secure covering for the spot. The last thing he'd wanted was for any predators nearby to be drawn to his cozy little hiding place by the smell of decomposition.

Squeaker had been moderately successful. He'd avoided that side of the porch after Moo died, partly from sadness and partly to distance himself from any unpleasant activity that might take place. But no intruders ever came.

Next door, at the house where he used to live, the chubby woman and her skinny husband moved into the apartment Jenna and her father had vacated.

A couple of times Squeaker had been spotted as he cut through their yard, and the chubby woman had shouted at him to 'get lost!' So in the main, Squeaker avoided that house, and the rest of the street beyond.

He had enough to contend with just patrolling the house next door, where he now lived and where Moo was buried, and the houses on the other side of it. As the days and then weeks passed, Squeaker developed a routine.

He would curl up in a sunny spot on the big covered porch once everyone in the apartments of the house had left for the day. Here, he would sleep. He dreamed, of course. Sometimes he dreamed of Jenna and Moo and in his dreams, that first period in his life took on an almost idyllic quality. His brain knew that it had been far from that, but he was sure that Jenna had cared about him and Moo. Now that he had no one, Jenna's affections seemed to outweigh the questionable treatment and accommodation he had received while with her and her father.

Squeaker sometimes dreamed of the dangers he had seen or encountered on the streets of the town where he was struggling to survive: the big metallic things the two leggeds drove along the smooth black roads, several large and unfriendly neighborhood dogs who had chased him away from their territories, and even rat traps near the stream that paralleled the street where he lived. He'd had the good fortune to spot the traps before stepping in any of them by mistake, but they were frightening.

One night, he had a very peculiar dream: a Tortoiseshell cat—he had never met her, or even seen such a cat in real life—appeared and seemed to be telling him something. She said to watch for a very special lady. It wasn't a warning, it seemed like more of an opportunity. The cat had seemed sad, and all Squeaker remembered when he woke up was a feeling of having been given something.

But as far as he could see, everything was pretty much the same as it had been for weeks: the little corner of the wraparound porch where he'd found a cozy place to sleep during the day among some boxes, and Moo's grave under the far side of the porch.

Squeaker's routine continued: each evening when night drew near and the two leggeds returned to the house, he would quietly disappear, and go hunting. He eluded notice for quite a long time this way.

Squeaker covered a fairly wide range for a kitten: about a square half-mile. In the gardens behind the houses on his street he often caught mice, both house mice and field mice, for the town was in a rural area, and farmlands were quite close.

He also learned how to get into the two leggeds' unsecured garbage once they had placed it curb side on pick up day. Sometimes those big dogs barked, and chased him away, but he usually managed to snare something to fill his belly. He had watched the way in which a pair of friendly-looking raccoons had burgled the garbage sacks, and when he encountered them again one very early morning, he approached them.

"*Hello*," he mewed.

The two raccoons, who had dug a small hole in a large black plastic garbage bag near the curb of a house down the street, turned.

"*Well-a, hello!*" they chorused.

Their accent was peculiar, but Squeaker understood them all right.

"*We didn't-a know your sort-a spoke!*" the raccoons continued. One paused in his investigation of the garbage bag, but the other returned to digging.

"*What are you doing?*" Squeaker asked curiously.

The raccoons explained that many two leggeds, though not all, put their garbage out the night before if pickup was very early. "*If-a dey use garbage-a cans, it's a bit-a more comp-a-li-cated, because-a many of dem a-lock,*" the raccoon explained. "*But if-a dey just put out-a da bags, well, we can a-smell if dere's anything good-a inside an' a-dig a hole an' a-see what we can a-find.*" He paused. "*It-a been a harsh winter, an' a-free range-a pickings are a-scarce.*"

"*Free range?*" Squeaker asked, not quite understanding.

"*Si. You a-know: field a-mice an' a like-a dat,*" the raccoon explained. "*You live 'round here?*" he queried.

Squeaker vaguely replied that he lived a few doors down, and the raccoon did not press him for more detail. Out on the streets, foraging animals might be friendly, but they all protected their home turf instinctively.

"*Look, look-a what I found!*" the other raccoon crowed gleefully, dragging a crumpled fast food bag out of the garbage spilled from the hole their sharp claws had made in the garbage sack. Inside the paper bag was a half eaten chicken sandwich and some fries.

Squeaker's mouth watered at the smell: the castoffs couldn't have been more than a few hours old, possibly the remnants of someone's unfinished dinner. Such a waste!

The two raccoons immediately began to portion out the sandwich and the fries: they had obviously done this before and had a system.

"My name's a-Prrrruuut an' a-dis is-a my brother, Kkkkkiiikkit," the first raccoon said around a mouthful of fries.

"Pleased to meet you," Squeaker replied politely. *"My name is—well, the little girl who used to take care of me called me Squeaker,"* Squeaker said. He hoped his drooling wasn't too obvious, and that the raccoons couldn't hear his stomach rumbling with hunger.

"Used to?" put in the other raccoon, who had pulled the lettuce and tomato out of the sandwich and was having himself a little salad.

"Yes." Squeaker nodded sadly. *"They moved away."*

"And they-a left-a you?" Kkkkkiiikkit exclaimed, horrified.

Squeaker nodded again.

"We see dat a lot," Prrrruuut noted grimly. *"I truly don't-a know what-a de two leggeds are a-tinking some-a-times: do dey a-tink domesticated animals will-a 'be all right' if-a dey leave a-dem behind, on-a dere own?"* he asked in rhetorical disgust.

"*Well, I've tried to do all right,*" Squeaker murmured. He wasn't boasting, but he didn't want these raccoons to think he was a sissy.

"*How long ago did-a dey leave?*" Kkkkkiiikkit asked.

Squeaker thought for a minute. Then,"*the big pine trees were in lots of two leggeds' houses with lights and shiny things,*" he began.

"*Christ-a-mas!*" chorused the raccoons. "*Dat's-a nearly a-two months. An' a-you've-a survived on your own dat-a long?*" Kkkkkiiikkit asked. He'd finished his salad and was now starting on a piece of chicken.

Squeaker nodded again, but more sadly. His orange ears drooped as he explained about his brother, Moo, and about the way they had been abandoned, and then thrown out, and how ill Moo had been, and how he had died. "*I couldn't help him,*" Squeaker admitted.

If he'd been able to weep, he would have. He missed his brother all the time, despite the fact that Moo hadn't been great company. But at least he'd been someone. And despite the lengthening days and the strengthening sunlight, every morning brought the fresh realization to Squeaker that he was a seven month old kitten on his own, living outside in the winter, at the mercy of just about anything larger and meaner than himself. And those were many.

"*Well, of-a course-a you a-couldn't a-help-a your brodder,*" Prrrruuut noted supportively. "*Your two leggeds should-a-taken you both to de vet.*" His tone was censorious, and Squeaker drew back a little. He hoped the raccoons weren't angry at him!

"*Oh, I'm a-not a-upset wid-a you, Master Squeaker,*" Prrrruuut said then, reading the little cat's mind. "*I'm a-upset-a wid de two leggeds.*" He shook his head. "*Dey want-a companion animals, but don't-a realize, or don't-a bodder to make, de commitment needed to keep-a them healthy.*"

"*There oughtta be a law!*" exclaimed Kkkkkiiikkit, chiming in. Then he held out a piece of chicken. "*Here, Master Squeaker. Have-a some dinner,*" he said, urging the chicken on the cat.

"*Really?*" Squeaker asked, and licked the drool from his lips. "*Thank you, oh, thank you!*"

After that encounter, Squeaker began to patrol the garbage bags set out the evening before collection day, but he stuck to the opposite side of the street, which the raccoons said was not their territory. Luckily, it didn't seem to be anyone else's, either, although a couple of times Squeaker found the garbage bags had already been broken into by the time he got there.

Still, the items he gleaned in this way—leftovers from casseroles, pizza and fast food meals mostly—supplemented the mice he could catch and kept him from starving.

One time he smelled a roast chicken. Some of the meat was gone, but there was a significant amount still on the bones, since whoever had eaten the chicken seemed to have only wanted the white meat. This provided Squeaker with a very satisfying meal. There was so much left that he was able to carry a whole leg and thigh back across the street to where he suspected Kkkkkiiikkit and Prrrruuut were foraging, and present them with the gift.

"*For-a us?*" Kkkkkiiikkit asked, pleased and surprised.

Squeaker nodded. "*There's too much for me, and I wanted to return your kindness,*" he said solemnly.

Now, it was full morning and Squeaker was just returning from a successful night of hunting. He planned to curl up in a sunny patch on the porch, as usual. But since the sunny patches kept moving, which he didn't really understand, this morning he'd crossed the front path, on his way to the far side of the porch which was now bathed in sunlight.

And so it was that the young woman saw him, and stopped in her progress to her front door, and spoke to him.

Chapter Nine

"Come here, kitty," she cooed, and bent down, holding out one gloved hand.

Squeaker, despite everything, was still a friendly cat, and still liked the two leggeds. So he approached, but cautiously, for his weeks on the streets had taught him that caution was wise.

"I won't hurt you, come here, sweetie," the young woman insisted.

"*Hello,*" Squeaker mewed.

"Why, what a funny meow you have!" the young woman exclaimed. "What's your name?" she asked.

Squeaker really didn't want to tell her his name, so he just looked up at her. His fur had come in very thick in response to the cold winter temperatures he'd been living in, and the young woman reached out to stroke him on his head, gently.

It had been weeks and weeks since a two legged had touched him. He'd been yelled at a couple of times when he'd been caught going through garbage, or seen late at night, patrolling for mice. But he hadn't been stroked, or petted, or held, it seemed, for ages.

He instinctively butted the young woman's hand with his head, squeezed his chartreuse colored eyes shut with pleasure, and started to purr.

"Oh, you're a friendly one, aren't you?" she murmured. Her fingers moved from his head down to his neck, where she felt for a collar. "Don't you belong to anyone, sweetie?" she asked. "You look like one of the kittens who used to live next door. But the family moved, and..."

Squeaker looked down. "*I am one of those kittens,*" Squeaker replied sadly. "*The other was my brother, and he died. They left us behind when they moved. No one wants me,*" he said quietly.

The young woman laughed lightly then. "Geez, that almost sounded like you can talk! And that's quite a purr you've got there..." She stood. "Well, I have to get inside to my apartment," she explained, heading for the front door once more. "I've got a kitty, too," she spoke in a conversational tone.

"*I know,*" Squeaker said. Was it possible this young woman understood him? It almost seemed like they were having a conversation.

The young woman laughed again. "Her name is Tuesday, because I adopted her from the Humane Society on a Tuesday, and it just seemed to fit!" she declared, smiling.

Squeaker tried to smile back, even though cats' mouths aren't made for such an expression.

"Okay, well, I think I'll call you Purrbot, 'cause you purr so much," the young woman said merrily. "I'll see you later," she said, as she unlocked the door and slipped inside. She deftly closed the door so Squeaker couldn't go in with her, but she did it gently.

Squeaker continued his routine after that, but now he made a point of not only lingering near the front path when he knew the young woman would be coming home from work, he also tried to find her cat, Tuesday.

She had been the grey tabby he and Moo had seen in the window at Christmas, he realized. Although Tuesday and the young woman had an apartment on the ground floor, the windows were several feet up from the ground, and Squeaker could not figure out how to jump to them.

However, there was more than one window in their apartment, of course, and while Tuesday favored the living room windows in which Squeaker and Moo had first seen her, and where her cat bed was, she too followed the sun around the house, just as Squeaker followed the sun around the porch.

Thus it was that one sunny morning when the young woman had already come home from work, Squeaker noticed a familiar shape in the window next to the porch rail. The porch wrapped around the entire house, but stopped at the chimneys on either side, and began again after the brick of the exterior chimneys had been cleared. The porch had been designed to fold in behind and in front of the chimneys. This meant that the porch rail here was at right angles to the rest of the rail.

Squeaker jumped up to the flat top of the railing and walked over as close as he could get to the window.

"*Hello,*" he meowed.

The grey tabby in the window narrowed her eyes at him and swished her tail. "*Who are you?*" she asked in a supercilious tone.

"*I'm—well, your two legged calls me Purrbot,*" he admitted. "*I don't have another name, really.*" Jenna had called him Squeaker. But Jenna was gone.

"*Oho! So you're the kitty I've smelled on her lately,*" Tuesday replied, relaxing. "*I think I've heard you around, too—you sleep on the porch, don't you?*"

Squeaker nodded. *"Yes. I'm very grateful no one has shooed me away,"* he added humbly.

Tuesday licked her shoulder twice, which in cat kinesthesiology is equivalent to a shrug. *"The two leggeds don't use the porch in winter, silly. But once the weather's nice, they will, and they probably won't want you around then,"* she told him declaratively.

Squeaker swallowed. This porch and this house wasn't much, but it was his home. If the two leggeds drove him off, where would he go?

"Maybe—maybe one of the two leggeds will adopt me," Squeaker suggested.

Tuesday shrugged again. *"Maybe."*

"Maybe your two legged will," Squeaker went on boldly. *"She's awfully nice to me when I see her coming home from work,"* he added.

Tuesday licked a paw and passed it assiduously over one ear and her whiskers. *"She's nice to everyone. She's a very kind two legged. But I don't think she will adopt you, Purrbot,"* she told Squeaker. *"For one thing, cats are solitary beings, and I quite like having my Staff all to myself, thank you very much. And secondly, there's a one pet limit per apartment in this house. Your best bet is that the two leggeds on the second floor take you in: they're the only ones without a pet."*

"Oh." Squeaker was very disappointed. *"Are they nice?"*

Tuesday shrugged again. *"Seem to be. Two guys, they work at some mall, I've heard them talk about it. I'm not sure what a mall is, but I think it's a place with a lot of places where the two leggeds can buy things."* She paused. *"One of them always smells of hamsters and such. He makes me hungry,"* she added, explaining that the two guys as well as the rest of the residents in the house were all friends with her two legged, and had all attended her Christmas party.

"I saw you that night," Squeaker told Tuesday, remembering. *"Moo—he was my brother, but he died —and I were watching from our house over there,"* he explained, gesturing with a shift of his eyes. *"You were in the window, and everyone looked so happy."* His voice was tinged with envy and sadness.

Tuesday didn't know what to say to that, so she was silent. She decided to wash the other side of her face.

"What other animals live here?" Squeaker asked a minute later, curious.

Tuesday told him about the golden retriever who lived on the second floor at the back, the iguana that lived on the third floor, and the small dog called a 'Papillon' who lived on the third floor front.

"She's no bigger than I am," the tabby said of the Papillon, *"and her two legged carries her around in a big leather handbag, and the Papillon has the most ridiculous bows and ribbons in her fur. Her two legged does that, too,"* Tuesday said derisively. *"You won't catch me letting any two legged do that to me,"* she declared.

"But—you have a necklace, Tuesday," Squeaker pointed out politely.

Tuesday frowned for a second, her green eyes on this small orange interloper. Then, her face cleared. *"Oh, you mean my collar!"* She smirked.

"This isn't a necklace. It's a collar, Purrbot. It means I belong to someone."

Chapter Ten

Tuesday's words stuck in Squeaker's head, and for days he wondered what it might be like to 'belong' to someone. To wear a handsome leather collar, as she did, with shiny medals on it.

She had explained that the round metal disks were her identification tag and her insurance tag, so that if she ever got lost, whoever found her would know to call the young woman, so they could be reunited.

But Tuesday had said she had no intention whatsoever of running away, even if she were given the opportunity. She had been a 'street kitty' too, without a home, until she'd been collected and brought to the Humane Society. That was where the young woman had found her, and adopted her.

'*Now that I have a real home, and Staff of my very own,*' Tuesday had declared, '*I would never do anything to jeopardize that, and I would never leave my Staff,*' she had finished.

Squeaker had considered the two options: being an inside kitty with no real opportunity to run and roam at will and yet 'belonging' to a loving, caring two legged, or being out on your own, alone, able to hunt and patrol as you chose but having no one to look out for you and keep you safe. Of the two, although he was doing his best under the latter circumstances and had only a flawed version of the former circumstances to refer to, he thought he would prefer the former. Preferably with a two legged like Tuesday's.

'*Why do you call your two legged your Staff?*' Squeaker had asked curiously.

Tuesday had drawn herself very tall and straight and looked at Squeaker seriously. '*Because, young Purrbot, if you do not train your Staff properly to know that your welfare is the highest priority, it never ends well,*' she had advised. '*But you must do it with a light and gentle paw, so they continue to believe that they are in charge,*' she had added, with a self-satisfied smirk.

Squeaker had just stared at Tuesday in amazement through the window. He could not imagine a two legged who thought that his welfare was even as important as theirs, never mind more important. The grey tabby, however, seemed to have adapted beautifully to her 'forever home,' as she called it, and accepted her food, her treats, her toys, her bed, and her 'Staff's' indulgence as her due.

Chapter Eleven

Within a day, the kind young woman began to put two little bowls out on the side of the porch that was sunny where she knew Squeaker—or Purrbot as she called him—would stay during the day. In one bowl she poured fresh water and in the other she put what she said was 'extra' food. It was mostly kibble, but often it was mixed with some wet food of varying types.

Squeaker didn't care what it was, he was grateful, and gobbled everything right up. He was particularly thankful for the fresh water, because he usually had to drink snow melt, and it was often dirty and didn't taste very good.

On a couple of very cold nights when the temperature dipped into the single digits and below, the kind young woman even invited Squeaker into the apartment she shared with Tuesday. Her place was quite large, and she had a half bath/laundry room where she fixed up a box with an old, but clean and soft blanket. On the first evening when plunging mercuries were forecast, she came out onto the porch early, and called to Squeaker.

He came running, as he had just started to roam for the evening, and so was nearby. And of course, he knew the name she had given him.

The kind young woman picked Squeaker up gently and quickly brought him into her apartment and into the half bath, and shut the door. Then she put him down on the vinyl floor.

"You're going to bunk here tonight, Purrbot," she whispered. "It's way too cold for you to be outside," she added considerately.

Squeaker looked around: on one side of the room, next to the washing machine and dryer, was the box with the lovely blanket. Next to that were two bowls, one with food and one with water. There was a window with café curtains, and he could easily fit behind the lower one to sit on the windowsill and look out. And on the other side of the room, next to the two legged style toilet, was a litter box. He knew what that was, of course, and when the young woman showed it to him and plopped him in it, he scratched at the litter to show her he recognized it, and would be a good boy.

She left for work, then, and closed the door behind her. But Squeaker wasn't alone for long: Tuesday arrived shortly after her 'Staff' left, and settled down on the floor outside the half bathroom door.

"See, I told you!" Squeaker said to Tuesday triumphantly after they had exchanged greetings. *"Your 'Staff' might adopt me!"*

Tuesday put her head on her paws and sighed. *"Purrbot, Purrbot, she might, but here in this apartment, she is only allowed one animal companion, as I told you. And that, you see, is me!"*

"Well, maybe she'll ask some friends to adopt me," Squeaker insisted.

"Maybe, young Purrbot."

Although the kind young woman did not adopt Squeaker, or Purrbot, after a few more cold nights where she allowed the little cat to come into her half bathroom while she went to work, she couldn't bear to turn him out again, even though the temperatures had moderated.

So she came up with a solution, which she told Tuesday one morning as they shared breakfast time. Squeaker had already been let outside for the day, even though the clouds presaged snow by afternoon.

"I wish I could keep him, he's a cutie," the kind young woman, whose name was Laura, told Tuesday. Laura was sitting at a small wooden table in her cozy kitchen, and Tuesday was sitting next to her food and water bowls. She had finished breakfast, and was washing her face.

"*He's all right*," Tuesday replied grudgingly, licking a paw.

"You like him, I know you spend all night chatting with him through the door," Laura continued with a grin. She took a bite of her toast and chewed purposefully.

"*Well, for a kitten, he's not bad*," Tuesday admitted. "*But you can only have one animal*," she reminded Laura.

"I can only have one pet, though," Laura ruminated.

Not for the first time, Tuesday wished her Staff could understand her better: it would save a lot of repetition in their conversations.

"But, here's my plan, Tuesday," Laura continued brightly. She scooped up a forkful of scrambled eggs, chewed and swallowed. "I'm going to ask Mr. Genser the landlord if I can keep Purrbot, if he only comes in at night. And even then, maybe just in the winter. What do you think of that?" she asked Tuesday.

Tuesday licked her shoulder twice and said nothing.

"That way, I can be sure Purrbot is safe, get him a collar and tags and I might even microchip him if he's going to be an indoor-outdoor kitty," Laura continued, planning aloud. She took a couple of mouthfuls of tomato juice, then ate a second bite of eggs.

"And when he's in at night, or whenever, he wouldn't be confined to the half bath, would he?" Tuesday asked. Her tone was both hopeful and melancholy. If 'Purrbot' became even an indoor-outdoor cat in their home, she would have to share her Staff, and her apartment, and Tuesday would need time to adjust to that idea.

"What, you don't think Mr. Genser will go for the idea?" Laura asked Tuesday.

"That's not what I said," Tuesday replied with a sigh.

"Well, I'm not sure, either, but all I can do is ask," Laura concluded. "I've checked at work, too, and no one is interested in adopting a kitty," she added sadly.

With another sigh, Tuesday made for the sunniest window to have a good snooze, and Laura handled the breakfast dishes and headed for her bedroom. She was off the following day, and planned to ask her landlord about Purrbot then.

Mr. Genser was even less enthusiastic about Laura's plan than Tuesday had been: he told Laura 'no' and even said that he really didn't want stray cats hanging around his apartment house.

"Well, then, I'll just have to call the Humane Society," Laura said sadly when she returned to her apartment after speaking with the landlord, who lived across from her on the ground floor of the huge old house.

"*Where I came from?*" Tuesday asked brightly. "*They were nice two leggeds, but there were a lot of cats.*"

"Yes, I'm sure you're pleased," Laura told Tuesday, sounding disappointed.

"*That's not what I said,*" Tuesday replied in protest, but twined her way around her Staff's ankles to show her she held her in high regard nonetheless.

Chapter Twelve

Laura called the Humane Society where she had found Tuesday, but they told her they were not accepting any cats at the moment, as they were full.

"Your best bet is to find a foster until the cat can be placed," the lady on the other end of the telephone said. She was sympathetic, but firm.

"But he's been outside for, oh, I don't know, all winter, I'm sure, and he really needs to be taken care of properly," Laura insisted. "I think he was one of two kittens who were abandoned by the people next door, when they moved," she added, voicing her suspicions. As she had come to know Squeaker, the awful truth of what probably had happened to him had dawned on her. It was such a foreign concept to her, though, it had taken a while for her to realize it.

If only, she thought, Purrbot could tell her!

"I don't know where the other kitten is," she added softly. "I haven't seen him."

The lady on the phone hemmed and hawed and then said, "here, why not call this Humane Officer," and read off a name and a number. "She works out of the next county and although they don't have a shelter in that county, she knows someone who runs a small private Rescue. I don't know if they have room, but they might. Can't hurt to try."

Laura called immediately and was gratified when the Humane Officer from the neighboring county answered. She explained the situation, and the Officer asked for details like Laura's address as well as the address of the house next door.

"I can contact the owner of that building and see who used to rent that apartment," the Officer told Laura, "and if we can find out where they are, we can charge them with cruelty and abandonment. That's a felony, so they're looking at fines, or jail time."

"Wow," Laura said. "Good. But meanwhile, the kitten—?"

"Oh, I'll call The Cat Ladies' Rescue and see if they can take him. If so, I can come get him at your convenience," the Officer replied cheerily.

Laura giggled at the name of the Rescue but agreed with alacrity. They made arrangements for the Officer to stop by that evening, and Laura ran outside to locate Squeaker.

"Purrbot!" she called softly. She didn't want Mr. Genser to know the kitten was still around. But she would let him know she had contacted the Humane Society. "Purrbot!" she called again, tramping through the mushy snow in the yard next to the big old house.

"*Here I am!*" came Squeaker's reply. He'd just been a yard or two over, in the shrubbery, stalking a mouse. Now that he was being fed good food on a regular basis, however, the activity had become more of a game and less of a necessity. Much of his natural playfulness, which had been shunted aside in favor of basic survival, was beginning to return.

He bounded over the snow to Laura's side.

"Let's go in now, even though it's early," Laura told Squeaker, and picked him up, carrying him in to his usual place in the half bath.

"*It's so nice in here,*" Squeaker sighed as his paws hit the vinyl flooring in Laura's half bath. "*It's warm and cozy, and there's a window to look out, and Tuesday talks to me so I'm never bored,"* Squeaker continued as he trundled over to the blanket and sat down.

"I asked the landlord if I could keep you," Laura began, and Squeaker's heart leapt for joy. "But he said no."

Squeaker's head drooped. *"I know, there's a one animal rule here,"* he murmured. *"It's all right. Thank you for trying. It's nice to be wanted,"* he added.

"Oh, sweetie, I didn't stop there, though: I called the Humane Society where I got Tuesday, but they're full and can't take you. So then I called the next county over: they have a Humane Officer but no shelter."

"Oh. How will that help?" Squeaker asked, confused.

"They work with a private Rescue, and I already spoke to the Officer, and she thinks they might have room for you!" Laura told Squeaker. "That way you'll be safe and warm and fed and..." Laura broke off, her eyes welling suddenly.

Squeaker, though, felt considerably cheered by this information, for although he was not sure what a Humane Officer was, he knew what a Rescue was: a place where unwanted and abandoned animals would be safe and cared for until they could be find a forever home.

Squeaker looked up at Laura and was surprised to see her eyes leaking. She was sad. Why?

"I'm going to miss you, Purrbot," Laura sniffed. "But I know that if the Rescue takes you, you'll be fine."

When the Humane Officer arrived at Laura's that evening, she praised Laura's efforts to look after the little orange cat. However, once she'd done her assessment on Squeaker—checking his eyes, his fur, his mouth, his litter box and squeezing him in peculiar places that made him yelp—she determined that his first stop should be the vet's.

"Goodbye, young Purrbot, and good luck!" Tuesday called as Squeaker was loaded into a large, secure carrier by the Humane Officer.

"Goodbye, Tuesday. It was great knowing you," Squeaker replied.

"Oh, I'll miss you too, Purrbot," Laura told Squeaker, running her fingers along the transport carrier's grate. Her eyes were leaking again.

"That's not what he said: he was talking to me!" put in Tuesday exasperatedly.

"Good luck teaching your two legged, I mean your Staff, to understand you," Squeaker told Tuesday.

"Thanks, young Purrbot. I'll need it," Tuesday replied grimly.

"Oh, see? Tuesday'll miss you too!" Laura exclaimed, scooping up her tabby cat and making her wave one of her paws at the carrier Squeaker was in.

"Well, yes, I will, I guess," Tuesday admitted, looking uncomfortable. *"But young Purrbot, don't you breathe a word of this,"* Tuesday continued, sounding insistent. *"She likes to make me wave good bye whenever two leggeds visit and then leave. I*

don't know why, I've said a proper farewell in my own way. I feel a fool."

Squeaker looked at them from the carrier's grating as the Humane Officer bundled him out of Laura's apartment. He would never forget the young woman's kindness to him, or Tuesday's friendship and advice.

"Don't feel a fool, Tuesday: she loves you," Squeaker called out. *"You're a lucky cat to have a two legged like that,"* he added.

He only hoped some day he was as lucky.

Chapter Thirteen

Squeaker's experience at the vet's wasn't an entirely happy one: no cat likes being poked and prodded, and since Squeaker had never had a checkup, not only did he have to have everything done, it was all new to him as well.

The vet, who happened to have evening hours that particular day and in any case worked closely with the Humane Officer, said Squeaker had ear mites, almost every intestinal worm there was, fleas, a couple of ticks, and was malnourished. An x ray picked up the remodeled fracture of his back leg, too, and the Humane Officer, learning of this, added another count to the charges she was preparing to file against the people who'd abandoned Squeaker.

Squeaker had inoculations in his hindquarters, fluids injected in his flank, got goop in his ears and between his shoulder blades, felt the veterinarian's instrument when the ticks came out, and had a pill forced down his throat. He liked the last thing least of all.

"You'll feel better soon," one of the veterinarian's assistants assured Squeaker as, slightly the worse for wear, he was placed in a large cage in a room with several other cages. There were two other cats and three dogs in more cages around the room.

In Squeaker's cage was the soft blanket from Laura's house, as well as the two dishes she had fed him from. There was water in one and a little bit of kibble in the other.

Squeaker's whiskers perked up when he smelled the familiar blanket, and, exhausted, he curled up and went to sleep, too tired to even be curious about the other denizens of the vet clinic.

The next morning, though, it was a different story. Squeaker woke early and polished off every morsel of kibble in his dish, and drank a lot of the water. His skin hurt in a few places, and he still couldn't hear too well because of whatever stuff they'd put in his ears, but he felt better. His resilience was quite astonishing and the vet techs as well as the Humane Officer would remark on it in the coming days.

Squeaker sat alertly up near the front of his cage, and watched as the other animals in the boarding room woke up.

"*Och, look, another cat,*" announced a scrappy-looking Terrier mix in a heavy accent when he noticed the new orange kitten. The Terrier was in one of the bottom cages on the other side.

"*Hello,*" said Squeaker.

"*Aye, and guid day to yew, young orange cat,*" the Terrier replied, not unkindly.

"*Goodness, what happened to you?*" Squeaker asked a moment later: he had spotted a colorful cast on the Terrier's right foreleg.

"*Och, broke me leash and ran in front of one of those horrid mechanical beasties,*" the Terrier replied. He sounded proud of himself, somehow.

"*Oh, yes, zey can be drrrreadful,*" a white miniature Poodle chimed in anxiously from one cage over. She stretched daintily. "*When my mistrrrress takes me on my leash I nevehr trrrry to brrrreak frrrree,*" she added in a righteous tone.

"Och, shush, now Suzie," the Terrier admonished with a shake of his head.

"My name is Suzette!" sniffed the Poodle, sounding hurt. She gave the terrier a reproachful look and then turned her back to him.

"Und mein Name ist Hans," said a distinguished looking older Doberman from the next cage. *"How do you do?"* he addressed Squeaker. His voice was very deep. *"Vat shall ve call you?"*

"I do very well, Sir," Squeaker replied politely. *"My, ummm, that is, the little girl I used to live with called me Squeaker,"* he told the Doberman, and the room at large, for everyone had stopped their morning ablutions to listen in.

Squeaker didn't mention that Laura and Tuesday had called him Purrbot: it seemed just as silly a name as Squeaker, and he felt that one silly name was quite enough. Honestly, he didn't know what his name should be, but he felt somehow that if he ever found a forever home, they would know what the right name for him was.

"Squeaker? That's a very odd name," murmured an elderly Himalayan cat from the cage next to Squeaker. *"Though, since two leggeds do not generally understand us well, I suppose your speech does sound like squeaks to them,"* she added ruminatively. She licked a paw, then passed that over her face.

"Sooooooo true!" chimed in a beautiful Calico with one gold and one green eye, from a cage at the far end of the row. She stretched carefully, then shook her piebald fur. *"I've heard tell of some two leggeds who <u>do</u> understand, and speak to us sensibly,*

though: none of this 'oh what a pretty kitty you are' nonsense. Of course we're pretty. Or handsome. We know that! Tell us something interesting, tell us something we don't know!" she exclaimed insistently, and paced across her cage, tail swishing.

"Like what?" the Himalayan queried. She seemed, though, to be smiling at the young Calico.

"Oh, I don't know: world events? How their day was at work? Maybe ask how mine was, even?" the Calico replied eagerly. *"And the names they come up with sometimes! You would hope they might give a bit more thought to them, but nooooo, it seems they pick the first bit of nonsense that comes into their heads: I mean, 'Squeaker'? I ask you!"* she finished in outrage on Squeaker's behalf. *"No offense,"* she added hastily.

"None taken," Squeaker returned. *"I did meet one two legged who seemed better at understanding us,"* Squeaker put in a moment later, thinking of Laura. *"But she usually got things wrong or backwards, anyway."*

The other animals laughed appreciatively.

Aside from Moo—who'd never talked much—the raccoons, and then Tuesday, Squeaker had never spoken with other animals. The birds around where he'd lived only ever spoke to each other, and all they had seemed to ever say was, *'cat! cat! danger! fly!'* And if the mice and other small rodents he'd chased in the old house's walls and in the underbrush had spoken, it had been in a dialect far too primitive for Squeaker to comprehend.

"So, what're ye in for, young Squeaker?" asked the Terrier, who said his name was MacDougal.

Squeaker told his tale, briefly, but affectingly enough that by the time he had finished, all the animals were sitting up, and nodding their heads sadly.

"You're lucky that young two legged cared enough to keep calling people until she found somewhere for you to be placed," noted the Himalayan sagely. She craned her neck out towards the bars on her cage as far as she could go, so she could see Squeaker. *"You're quite handsome—or you will be when you're cleaned up,"* she added, wrinkling her nose slightly. *"You'll find a forever home."*

"Do you have one?" Squeaker asked, curious. The Himalayan's name was Annapurrna.

The cat nodded complacently. *"Oh, yes. My Staff has owned me since I was a kitten. He gave me my name, which he says is a pun, because Annapurna is the name of a Himalayan mountain,"* she explained. *"And I am, of course, a Himalayan cat,"* she added, fluffing her fur and curling her tail around her back legs as she sprawled almost indolently on a soft cushion covered in cat printed material.

Squeaker wasn't quite sure what a pun was, or what mountains had to do with anything, but he nodded politely. Here, he thought, was another cat who referred to her two legged as her Staff. It must be the right thing to do.

"I am just here for my annual physical and dental cleaning," Annapurrna continued. *"My Staff will be here this afternoon to collect me!"* she announced with confidence.

The young Calico, whose name was Electra, explained she had just been spayed, and would be going home that afternoon as well. *"My Staff persons are professors at a local college,"* she told Squeaker, sounding quite proud of them. *"Classics—Greek and Latin language and literature. That's where my name comes from."*

As they all chatted together, Suzette the Poodle explained that she had been brought in for a routine checkup, and Hans was having his hip looked at.

"I am a senior citizen, und arthritis gets us, just like it gets ze two leggeds," Hans rumbled. *"I do not like ze cortisone injections, but zey help,"* he added, sounding resigned.

"I had a bunch of injections," Squeaker murmured sympathetically. *"I didn't like them much."*

Squeaker was to discover later that morning that he liked baths even less than being given a pill or getting injections. But once he was dried and combed, and then had thoroughly licked himself clean all over and arranged his fur properly, he had to admit, he felt much better.

"So where are you going, once you're recovered, I mean?" asked Electra curiously. They had all been fed lunch, and were now waiting to be discharged, or planning to spend the remainder of the afternoon resting and chatting amongst themselves.

"The lady who, well, who saved me, I guess, her name was Laura," Squeaker began. *"She and the Humane Officer said I was going to a Rescue,"* he replied.

"*Och, aye, I ken what they be!*" MacDougal responded enthusiastically. "*Next best thing to a forever home,*" he added, and nodded decisively.

"*Ach, yes, you are kept safe, und varm, und fed, und ze two leggeds at ze Rescue try to find you a goot, forever home,*" Hans agreed. "*Und if not, you stay at ze Rescue. But you vill neffer be—vell, ve do not like to speak of it,*" he murmured diffidently.

"*What he wants to say is, you'll never be killed if they run out of room,*" Annapurrna finished in soft voice. "*A lot of shelters, unless they are truly 'no kill' shelters, do that, you know, young Squeaker.*" She paused. "*You really are extremely lucky, if you've been given a spot in a Rescue.*" She paused again. "*Maybe you should change your name to Lucky!*"

Squeaker was still trying to process the concept of killing healthy and probably young animals because a shelter was overcrowded. "*But—why is there no room? Why are there so many unwanted animals?*" he asked of no one in particular.

Hans sighed, and put his muzzle between his big tan and black front paws, looking dejected. "*Because ze two leggeds do not alvays bozzer to neuter us, und zo, zere are more and more puppies und kittens born, und not enough homes for zem all.*"

Squeaker was shocked into silence. "*But—that's irresponsible,*" he concluded. "*And—it's murder!*" he breathed, looking almost pleadingly from the Himalayan to the Calico to the Doberman to the Poodle to the Scottie, as though hoping someone would say it wasn't true.

But no one did. They all just hung their heads and were silent for several long seconds.

"*If only the two leggeds would value our lives as much as they do their own, perhaps things would be different,*" ventured the Calico in a soft voice. "*My Staff persons do. But not everyone does. And there are even low cost programs to help people on fixed or low incomes with the cost of neutering their pets,*" she added informatively. "*Of course, I don't think two leggeds should adopt an animal if they can't afford one,*" she added censoriously. "*But that's a different problem.*"

Suzette the Poodle weighed in. "*I hearrrr on ze news all ze time zat two leggedz kill ozzer two leggedz. I zink zey do not value life, any life, much, at all,*" she finished *sadly*. "*Parrrrrticularrrrly animal livessss.*"

"*I say a prayer every night for all the animals in the shelters and on the streets, the ones who don't have forever homes, or a place in a Rescue,*" Annapurrna said quietly.

Squeaker blinked. "*I think that's a fine idea, Annapurrna,*" he told her. "*I'm going to do that, too.*" He paused. "*After all, if it weren't for Laura and the Humane Officer, I'd still be one of them.*"

Chapter Fourteen

Squeaker remained at the vet clinic for a few more days, and the animals who were there initially were discharged, and new animals brought in. Most were friendly, and Squeaker was not lonely or bored while he continued to recover.

The kind veterinarian and the vet techs also played with Squeaker a little bit, and petted him, whenever they came to check on him. Finally, his health had improved enough for him to be neutered, and then the Rescue would accept him.

The operation barely took fifteen minutes and hurt less than the light anesthesia injection Squeaker was given. When he came fully awake, his hind end was a bit tender, but since he was just eight months old, he didn't feel much of anything else.

A couple of days later, Squeaker was once more checked over by the vet, and then pronounced healthy and ready to go. He was loaded into a different carrier that smelled of bleach and had a faded, but clean, towel in the bottom of it. The little bowls he'd had at Laura's and the blanket she'd given him were left behind as he headed for a new chapter in his life.

He felt sad, and a little bit frightened as he was brought to the front of the office. What would happen next?

A kind looking lady took the carrier from the vet tech, and put her face right up to the grating on the carrier's door.

"Oh, aren't you handsome," she cooed.

Squeaker turned and looked at her, and sniffed tentatively. She smelled of soap, and flowers. *"Thank you for the compliment,"* he replied. *"Are you my new, erm, Staff?"* he asked.

The lady just kept smiling, her warm hazel eyes twinkling with friendliness. "Well, you just come along with me." She stood up then. "What kind of name is Purrbot?" she exclaimed, looking at the hand written memo she'd been given.

The vet tech shrugged. "That's what the woman who called us, who found him as an abandoned stray, told us she called him," he explained.

The lady, whom the vet tech called 'Judy' sighed, and looked at the memo again. "Well, I can't call him that: it's silly!"

Squeaker agreed from his carrier.

"Oh, it says here he was found on Wyatt Street," Judy continued, still reading the note. "I can call him Wyatt," she said decisively. "At least that's a name." She bent down and looked into the carrier. "Ok? Wyatt?"

Squeaker purred and rubbed his whiskers on the grating of the door. *"It's a lot better than Purrbot or Squeaker!"* he agreed happily, even though it still didn't seem like quite the right name for him. But it would do.

"Let us know if you have any trouble, but he seems pretty healthy in spite of everything," the vet tech told Judy. "Oh, and we heard from the Humane Officer: she filed the charges, but the people left no forwarding address and no one seems to know where they were going, so it's unlikely they'll ever be found, and made to answer for what they did to—erm—Wyatt," he said, peeking over to smile into the carrier at the orange cat. "He had a really rough start, but he's doing great now."

And in a few more minutes, Squeaker—now called Wyatt—was in another vehicle, on his way to the Cat Ladies' Rescue.

The lady called Judy, as well other ladies called Sara and Paula, and a few of their friends, ran the Rescue, which is how it got its name, 'Cat Ladies' Rescue.' They took in strays, unwanted and abandoned cats, and ferals when they could catch them. They got them neutered if need be, and made sure they were healthy, and then sought to place them in forever homes if they were adoptable. However, Judy and her friends had become so fond of the Rescue's residents, they never really minded if their cats didn't get placed immediately.

It was a labor of love to keep the Rescue going, and neighbors and the community helped, too. Donations of food, litter, cleaning supplies, blankets and the like were always showing up at the Rescue's door, and the owner of the building where the Rescue was located allowed it to occupy the premises rent free. Others donated money or services and Judy and her friends did their part to ensure that the Rescue was scrupulously clean, and that the cats had everything they needed. More than a score of litter boxes were scooped twice a day, food and water bowls washed and re-filled, floors swept daily and washed weekly, along with countless other jobs that needed to be done to maintain the Rescue well.

Squeaker/Wyatt arrived in the middle of the day when the cats at the Rescue were mostly asleep. As Judy carried him in, he could smell many felines of all ages and both genders, but he didn't have time to say hello to anyone.

Judy placed him in an upper cage in a large room at the back, and gave him food and water. The towel came with him, and a new, soft plushy blanket was also put in his roomy cage. Judy tucked a little felt mouse into the blanket: it made a crinkling noise when Squeaker/Wyatt touched it with a tentative paw. There was even a small litter box in one corner.

He would be kept in this isolation cage at the Rescue for a couple of days, to give the cats there a chance to adjust to him, and to allow him to be fully healed before he was allowed to mingle with the rest of the residents. Then he'd have the run of the Rescue, which consisted of several rooms and a long hallway.

Squeaker/Wyatt curled up towards the rear of his cage and wrapped his tail around his feet; one eye peeked over the tip of his tail, watching in case any of the residents wandered by. He hoped the cats here at the Rescue were friendly.

He noted with relief that the Rescue was nice and cozy and warm. It reminded him a little bit of Laura's laundry room and for a moment, he had a pang of loneliness. He missed Laura, and Tuesday. He wondered if they missed him, too. He was very thankful to Laura for making certain he was safe and off the streets.

"Ok, Wyatt, I'll see you tomorrow, and Sara will probably be in later to clean the boxes and check on everything, and give Snaps his meds, so you'll meet her then," Judy said cheerily. She shut off the overhead light, leaving just small night lights illuminating the big back room where Squeaker/Wyatt was. He heard her footsteps as she went back down the hall. Then he heard a few more indistinct words as she spoke to some of the resident cats in the front room. Then Squeaker/Wyatt heard the door to the Rescue open, and then close. The lock turned.

Chapter Fifteen

There was a silence of about two minutes, and then a couple of muffled thumps sounded in the room adjacent to the one Wyatt was in. His acute hearing picked up the sound of paws padding across the vinyl floor towards his cage. Then a moment later a cat addressed him from the floor in front of him.

"Well, hello there: who are you?"

Wyatt uncurled himself and walked deliberately to the front of his cage, and looked down towards the floor. A long, slender black and white cat was sitting on his haunches, looking up at Wyatt with interest and curiosity.

"I'm called Wyatt," Wyatt said politely. *"What's your name?"*

The cat blinked once: in cat language, a welcome, or a sign of friendliness. *"I'm called Oreo,"* he said genially.

Another cat, almost as slender as Oreo but not with the same coat color, trotted into the room at this point. She was a brown tabby with a few orange splotches here and there on her sleek fur and her right back paw was all orange.

"You talking to the new one?" she asked eagerly.

"Yes—this is Wyatt," Oreo said, making introductions. *"And Wyatt, this is my sister, Renesme."*

Renesme made a funny face that was half grimace half smile. *"It's after a character in some film the two leggeds like,"* she explained to Wyatt.

"It's a little, well, fancy, if you ask me. But they didn't."

"They don't ask, do they?" Wyatt agreed companionably, remembering Electra's diatribe against the silly names the two leggeds gave animals many times.

Renesme seemed to agree.

"Well, they don't understand our language," Oreo explained. "And they have no idea we understand them!" He paused. "Although, at least my name makes sense," he added, just a touch self defensively.

"What does 'o-re-o' mean?" asked Wyatt, and the cat explained that it was a type of cookie that the two leggeds liked to eat. It was white and black, just like his fur.

"So, you here to stay?" Renesme asked a moment later.

Wyatt licked his shoulder nervously. "I don't know. I'm not sure. That is, this is a Rescue, isn't it? I can stay here if I want, can't I?" His voice was anxious and just a bit beseeching.

"Oh, yeah, sure you can," Renesme answered promptly. "If that's what you want. But of course, we all hope to find a forever home," Renesme continued.

Wyatt was about to answer that as far as he was concerned, he was just grateful to be at the Rescue and wouldn't dream of wishing for anything more, but he was interrupted. A couple more thumps sounded from the next room and then some running paws, and three more cats entered, the last one skidding to a stop in front of Wyatt's cage and getting a batting around his ears from Renesme for his trouble.

"Watch it!" she scolded.

The other cat, an elegant black male, bowed his head briefly as though in apology, and then turned to Wyatt.

"Oh! A ginger boy!" he announced happily. *"We haven't had one of those for a long time,"* he added, blinking. *"Welcome to the Cat Ladies' Rescue...erm, what's your name?"*

"Wyatt," replied Wyatt.

"My name is Henry," the black cat said. *"I see you've met Oreo and Renesme,"* he continued. Then he introduced the two other cats who had arrived: Buffy and Shadow.

"Pleased to meet you all!" Wyatt said happily. They were quite friendly, and they looked well fed and groomed and healthy and taken care of. *"I'm looking forward to being able to greet you properly, when I am out of this cage,"* Wyatt added apologetically.

"No worries, Wyatt," responded Oreo authoritatively. *"Everyone is sequestered here for a day or two, just so we all get used to each other. You'll be out with us in no time."*

Oreo had been correct. Two days later, Wyatt—who now hardly ever remembered that Laura had called him Purrbot and Jenna had called him Squeaker—was allowed out of his cage and permitted to roam the Rescue's roomy areas freely. Renesme made introductions, but most of the cats had already introduced themselves.

Wyatt met Snaps, to whom Judy had referred that first afternoon. He was a handsome seal point Siamese who told Wyatt that he had been saved from being dumped at a shelter when his two leggeds had discovered that he had a medical condition.

"I have what they call 'liver shunt,'" he explained one morning after breakfast. *"It means that the blood bypasses my liver, so it never gets purified, and toxins can build up in my blood and make me ill."*

"You don't look ill to me," Wyatt offered.

Snaps' long black whiskers tilted up at the compliment. *"All I need to live a healthy life are antibiotics and a low protein diet,"* he explained, adding that the medication Sara gave him every day was the antibiotic. *"It tastes awful, but I've stopped fighting,"* he sighed. *"I know it keeps me healthy."*

"So why did you end up here?" Wyatt asked, confused. It didn't seem that the special diet and the medication was that big a deal, not if it kept Snaps healthy.

"My two leggeds didn't want to bother giving me medication every day, or feeding me a special diet," Snaps replied grimly. *"They said it was 'too much trouble,' and said they'd worry if they went away and a sitter had to take care of me."*

Wyatt was surprised, and sad to hear this, but said nothing.

"I could understand if they had been unable to afford the medication, or the special food," Snaps continued. *"But..."* he broke off. Then he licked one shoulder twice.

"Well, isn't it lucky you were discovered and brought here?" Wyatt had rejoined encouragingly.

Snaps had nodded. "Yes, indeed."

"Do you think you'll find a forever home?" Wyatt asked hopefully.

Snaps looked at him gravely from his sky blue eyes. "Anything is possible, Wyatt. But I doubt it. The two leggeds want kittens, they don't usually want older cats. And they surely don't want cats with health problems, even if they're easily treatable."

Wyatt hung his head in companionable sadness. What a shame. How short sighted the two leggeds could be, he thought. So many beautiful, wonderful cats who would make perfect companions, overlooked for such small issues.

Chapter Sixteen

Wyatt had been interested to learn that the cats at the Rescue were fed wet food every morning, into which some probiotics were sprinkled: this kept everyone healthy and given his prior intestinal issues, Wyatt was very glad of it. Dry kibble was available 24/7, which Wyatt thought a true embarrassment of riches.

Some of the cats at the Rescue were extremely timid, and hid almost all the time, and ran whenever Wyatt approached. Buffy explained that these had been feral cats, wild cats who had never known a home or the loving touch of a two legged.

"I was one of them, and I still hide up until I get to know new two leggeds," Buffy confessed one sunny March morning. He and Wyatt were side by side in one of the Rescue's large front windows. They were watching for Judy's car to arrive, as she usually did the morning shift.

"But these cats hide from _me_!" Wyatt replied, sounding a little sad. *"I'm a cat, like them. Why should they hide?"*

Buffy sighed. *"They don't know you yet. In time, they may not run, but they will always keep their distance. In them, the flight instinct is so deeply ingrained they will never really be comfortable in their own fur,"* Buffy noted.

"That's terrible!" Wyatt exclaimed.

Buffy nodded. *"Yes. But remember, the life they were born into is not this one."* He paused, and then directed Wyatt's attention towards a grey tabby cat with a white bib and big green eyes. *"See him? That's*

Brother. He's a big, grown up cat and yet he hides, and keeps to himself, even among us cats."

"*Why?*" Wyatt queried, not understanding.

"*Because inside he is still a tiny, frightened kitten all alone in the world."*

"*But I was a frightened kitten all alone in the world after my brother died,*" Wyatt replied. "*And I'm not afraid."*

Buffy chuckled, a deep sound like a purr. "*Well, you are made of different stuff than Brother is, young Wyatt,*" he replied. "*We are all different, just like the two leggeds, and just like all animals. Some can overcome their fears. You might have done so because you needed to, to survive. But others, well, they do not ever overcome that terror of the unknown, of the different, of those who are not the same as they are,*" Buffy explained.

"*D'you—d'you think he ever will?*" Wyatt whispered, watching Brother tip toe cautiously around a partition and slink down the hall towards the room where the food bowls were kept.

Buffy sighed. "*Probably not. Perhaps, if a two legged would adopt him as an only cat, and really have a lot of patience with him, perhaps, in time, he would come to trust again. But I do not know: such two leggeds are rare. Most have good intentions when they adopt a cat, but they expect a cat who is already socialized. Most will not be able to spend the amount of time and have the patience to wait for a timid feral cat to relax enough to trust, and to love."*

"*But you were a feral, and...*" Wyatt protested.

Buffy interrupted. "*Yes, I was, but the feral colony I belonged to was near a large farm run by two leggeds. I got to know them and learned that two leggeds can be ok. They fed the colony and got as many of us as they could neutered, and if one of us got ill, they took us to the vet."*

Wyatt made a funny face. *"I got 'neutered,'"* he informed the ginger American fold.

Buffy sighed once again. *"It's better, really, because there are so many that aren't, so there are too many kittens in the world and not enough forever homes."*

Wyatt nodded. He had experienced enough of what a forever home was <u>not</u> to have some idea of what it might be. He thought Tuesday had a forever home with Laura: she was a lucky girl. And he knew from the animals he'd met at the veterinarian's clinic, all about what happened in shelters when they were overcrowded. He had been faithful to what he'd told Annapurrna: he prayed for the animals in shelters and on the streets every single night before he curled up to go to sleep.

"Do you think we will ever find our forever homes?" Wyatt asked Buffy a few minutes later.

The older cat looked at him gravely from his round amber eyes. *"This Rescue is our forever home,"* he began slowly. *"If you mean a home with a two legged, or a family, where we are the only companion animal, or one of just a few who are highly cherished and whose two leggeds have made a commitment to us, well, perhaps. As I say, two leggeds who really understand that when you adopt an animal it's for life, not until it isn't convenient or until you move or until you have a child, well, those two leggeds are rare."*

Wyatt looked downcast.

"*But sometimes,*" Buffy rejoined, and turned to look out the window again, where Judy's car had just pulled up. "*Sometimes you find one. Or the two legged finds you.*"

Chapter Seventeen

As the days went by, Wyatt got to know all the cats at the Rescue. Brother's mother, MamaKitty, had three other grown kittens who were also residents. They had been born on the roof of an abandoned house and were all quite shy and very quiet.

Oreo and Renesme were the alpha cats, more or less, in the group. It was unusual to have so many cats all living together, but the Rescue was roomy enough that there were enough places to retreat and have some solitary time, as needed.

Buffy and Shadow, whom he had met on his first night, were both former ferals, as was a cousin of Shadow's, called Lemonie. She had been found on a local road with a similar name. Shadow had been found nearby, after someone had thrown her out of a moving vehicle. Her pelvis had been fractured, but it had healed, and now the only sign of the injury was that her tail often curled up over her back when she walked.

Wyatt told Shadow once he thought this made her very pretty, and Shadow, flattered, had blinked slowly at him.

"Why thank you," she had said. *"It hurt for a long time, but then it hurt less and less and now, it hardly hurts at all,"* she'd explained of her fractures. *"Sometimes on really rainy days, it aches a little. But I keep moving."*

"I fractured my back leg when the man I lived with shoved me into a wall," Wyatt had told her companionably.

"Oh, you poor thing!" Shadow had returned. *"Isn't it awful, the way some two leggeds treat us?"* she'd asked rhetorically. *"I am so grateful to be here: I'm safe. And they love us all, you know."*

Wyatt had nodded. *"I know."*

Princess Anne was a standoffish long haired grey Persian with a beautiful face and gorgeous green eyes, but she didn't like any of the other cats at the Rescue, even Wyatt! He had tried to say hello to her one morning, and she'd cuffed his ears for his trouble and she'd hissed.

But Princess Anne's life had been an horrific one, as Oreo explained to Wyatt one evening. Sara had been in to do the litter boxes and top up the food and water, and she'd played with everyone in the big front room for a while. But now she'd left, and the cats were settling down for the night. Oreo and Wyatt sat together on one of the large plush cat beds that dotted the floor in the back room. A snowstorm raged outside and some of the cats were sitting up in the front windows, watching the storm and tapping at the glass as the dancing flakes swirled and fell. But it was warm and cozy in the back room, and Oreo and Wyatt snuggled there, and started talking.

Oreo and Renesme had been tiny little kittens when they'd been rescued, Oreo explained, and Sara had fed them with a bottle for a couple of weeks until they could eat kitten food.

"Our mother had been hit by a car, and killed," Oreo told Wyatt.

"Oh, I'm so sorry!"

Oreo gave a philosophical shrug. *"I am too, but she was a stray, and we would have been strays, so* on balance, maybe this Rescue is all right. I like it when Sara plays with us. And there's a little girl, too, who comes some times, and I'm her favorite." He preened.

"Will she adopt you?" Wyatt asked eagerly. He'd be happy for his friend, even though he'd miss him.

"I doubt it. Her mother says they can't have a cat in their small apartment."

Wyatt nodded, and said he understood that.

"Anyway, we were so small that Princess Anne didn't really mind us too much, and she used to tell us stories sometimes about her life, and warn us not to trust the two leggeds," Oreo continued.

"Yes, I've noticed she isn't very affectionate, even with Miss Judy!" Wyatt put in.

Oreo nodded wisely. "Well, if I had suffered what Princess has, I'd be cautious too," he offered. Then he explained that Princess had been a stray near an apartment complex and she had been terrorized by a gang of young boys. "There's no other word for it," Oreo said in a low voice. "They shot at her with BB guns, and tried to cut off her tail!" he whispered.

Wyatt was shocked. "They WHAT?" Then: "no, no, don't repeat it. How could someone do that? Why?"

Oreo shrugged. "They called it sport, according to Princess." He paused. "I blame the parents. They don't give their children the proper respect for all life, including cats. Their values and priorities are all messed up and the kids grow up having no boundaries and no concept of right and wrong."

"What did Princess do? Did she attack them?" Wyatt asked, thinking that he thought that was what he would have done.

"She ran, and found her way to a store, I think it was, a little mini mart along the highway. They didn't want her hanging around, so they called the Humane Officer who came and got her, and brought her to the vet, and then called Judy to see if the Rescue would accept her," Oreo answered.

"Just like me!" Wyatt breathed. *"Well, I understand her better now, thank you,"* he told Oreo.

From then on, Wyatt gave Princess Anne a wide berth, and always dipped his head respectfully if they passed in the hallway.

Maya was a pretty long haired dilute calico with a lot of Persian in her blood. She was friendly, but didn't really pal around with anyone. Wyatt did learn from her, though, that she had once been someone's pet, but her two legged had died, and she'd been brought to the Rescue.

"I would love to find another home with a two legged," Maya told Wyatt longingly one day as they were side by side in the big window. *"But I don't know if I ever will. I'm older, you see: I'm five! And most two leggeds want a kitten. Older cats are usually really hard to find forever homes for,"* she murmured sadly.

"But five isn't old," Wyatt had countered. *"Many cats live to be fifteen, or even twenty! You have many years left."*

Maya had just nodded. *"Tell the two leggeds that."*

Chapter Eighteen

Henry, the elegant black cat, had also been a stray brought in by the Humane Officer. He was a little older than Maya and told Wyatt that when he and his two litter mates had been brought in, they had been kittens.

"My two litter mates—grey tabbies with white paws and bibs—got adopted when we had only been here about a month," he reminisced.

"They didn't take you, too?" Wyatt asked. *"Kittens are small: if you've got room for two, why not take all three?"* he murmured.

Henry sighed. *"I heard them say they didn't want a black cat,"* he told Wyatt.

Wyatt frowned. *"Why?"* He thought Henry was extremely handsome, and his solid inky fur coat made him look somehow debonair as well.

"The two leggeds think, well, some of them think, that black cats are bad luck. That's what these two leggeds said," Henry replied.

"Bad luck? That's ridiculous!" Wyatt exclaimed.

The two were lounging on top of an old desk that occupied a corner of the front room. Long ago, the building in which the Rescue was housed had been a veterinarian's office, and the desk was a remnant from those days.

Now, Henry extended one slender paw and stretched, flexing his claws. *"Well, yes, of course it is, Wyatt. It's as silly as saying that ginger cats are good luck, or that tabbies are intelligent, or that calicos are sneaky! That's all just what the two leggeds read into us. It's called 'anthropomorphizing,'*" he enunciated proudly.

Wyatt tried to repeat the word to himself, not too successfully. "*What does that mean?*" he asked.

"*It's when two leggeds decide on an animal's personality based on two legged personalities,*" Henry explained archly.

"*Why would they do that?*" Wyatt asked, frowning. "*We have our own personalities: we don't need theirs.*"

"*Because they really don't understand us,*" Henry replied. "*If they did, we could talk, and then they would know what we are truly like,*" he continued. He turned to look at Wyatt and his bright, slightly slanted green eyes were sparkling. "*Cats are just like anyone else: we are all different, with different motivations and needs and likes and dislikes,*" he explained. "*It's a rare two legged who can genuinely understand that and not let their own personalities get in the way.*"

"*How did you learn all of this,*" Wyatt asked. "*And that huge, long word?*"

Henry smirked. "*I keep these big ears open, and I listen when the two leggeds talk. Sometimes they do say things worth remembering although mostly it's a load of rubbish about food and the weather!*" he declared dismissively. "*But Judy had a friend here one day, and she was talking about some film she had seen with her grand daughter, and about how the film maker had anthropomorphized the animals in the film, and she thought it was all the film maker's own personality coming through in the animals.*"

Wyatt looked amazed, but nodded at his friend. *"I see."* He sighed. *"Some two leggeds seem to understand us better than others,"* he ventured.

Henry nodded. *"Yes. They do. But it takes an exceptionally sensitive two legged, and it takes time, to really be able for them to know what we are saying,"* he finished.

There were two other black cats at the Rescue: Hootie, a young semi long haired cat with huge green eyes—hence his name—and Melle, a petite female who loved to play. The Rescue had lots of toys and scratching posts for the cats to amuse themselves with, and Melle loved to chase strings and feathered toys and anything that moved. She and Renesme got into a squabble one day over a six inch long catnip stuffed banana. They solved the disagreement by tugging so hard on the toy that it split in two, so each had her own to play with. And the rest of the cats had a great time rolling around in all the loose catnip.

When Paula came in to clean that evening, she just shook her head and smiled, and swept up the mess.

Hootie was a friendly cat who loved other animals, especially dogs. To his sorrow, his two leggeds had brought him to the Rescue because he preferred the family dog's company to their own.

"Can you imagine anything sillier?" Renesme asked Wyatt one morning as they were discussing Hootie, who was currently occupying the top of a tall cupboard in the kitchen. *"Two leggeds should be jumping for joy if their cat likes their dog!"* she pronounced with a flick of her tail. *"I mean, it takes a*

big heart, to like those slobbery canines," she explained fastidiously.

Wyatt nodded his agreement. *"He's a very handsome cat,"* he put in of Hootie. *"I love his floofy tail."*

Renesme gave Wyatt a look, then washed a paw and passed it over her face. *"Well, I wish he'd find another home,"* she murmured. *"The two leggeds don't think we have feelings, but we do, and Hootie is taking that rejection very hard,"* she told Wyatt sympathetically.

Chapter Nineteen

One day after Wyatt had been at the Rescue about a week, he was introduced to Allie. She was a very elderly cat, nearly 20 years old, and all white. She had been declawed on all four paws by her original owners, but left behind when they moved.

Because Allie was fragile, Judy usually kept her in a small room by herself, but when she was there, Judy often let Allie out to say hello and play with the rest of the cats.

So one morning while Wyatt was busy at one of the many feeding stations Judy had just filled with fresh kibble, he heard the door to Allie's room open, and then he heard several of the cats he'd come to know and think of as his new friends, greeting the elderly cat.

She was, truly, the *grande dame* of the Rescue.

"*I hear there is a new boy here,*" Allie said in a soft, whispery sort of voice. "*I'd like to meet him,*" she said, and made her way on delicate paws towards Wyatt. It seemed the other cats parted for her as she processed slowly across the vinyl covered floor.

Wyatt had turned from the food bowl, and had hastily washed his whiskers, and then licked his paws clean.

"*How do you do, Ma'am,*" he said, sitting up straight on his haunches, and nodding slightly, the same way he nodded to Princess.

"*Hello, young one—they call you Wyatt I hear?*" Allie replied genially.

"*Yes, Ma'am,*" Wyatt replied. "*It is the name of the street where I was found,*" he added, recalling that Judy had said as much to the vet tech when she'd re-named him.

Allie regarded him from gentle blue eyes that both had a slight milky cast to them. *"You've very nice manners,"* she murmured. *"Who taught you those?"* she queried, curious.

Wyatt licked at one shoulder twice, quickly. *"I do not know, Ma'am,"* he answered honestly. *"I just speak the way it seems correct to me to speak,"* he added.

"Ah, well, gingers: the best temperament of any cat, if you ask me," murmured Allie. Then: *"The other cats tell me you were left behind when your people moved?"* Allie asked, and Wyatt nodded confirmation. *"The same happened to me,"* she said in a soft, sad voice. *"But Judy found me, scrounging for scraps outside the diner in town, and brought me here,"* she added, noting that she had been at the Rescue since Judy had begun it.

"And may I ask, Ma'am, I heard Henry say you had been declawed?" Wyatt asked.

"That is true, Wyatt." She offered one oddly soft paw to him for inspection.

"Do you know why your two legged family did that to you?" Wyatt whispered, peering at her paw. *"Henry explained to me what it is, and it sounds horrible! Why would anyone do that?"*

He couldn't help himself asking Allie the question. It had bothered him ever since Henry had clued him in as to who was in the special room and what her story was. Wyatt found many of the things the two leggeds did unfathomable, but some, like declawing, were downright cruel.

Unlike the atrocities Princess had suffered, it had been adult two leggeds who had declawed Allie. So their actions couldn't be explained away by saying they were too young to know any better, because no one had taught them respect.

Allie hung her head, then washed one ear in a haphazard manner. For a moment, Wyatt wasn't sure she had heard him: white cats had notoriously bad hearing, and some were totally deaf. Although Allie could hear, her advanced age might mean she didn't hear very well, he thought.

But Allie had heard. She was just formulating her reply.

"Like all cats," she began in a reminiscent tone, *"I like to claw things. It is good exercise, and it sharpens my claws, and most importantly, it leaves my scent signature on items, to say, 'this is mine,' and let other cats know,"* Allie explained.

Wyatt nodded. He knew that. He himself enjoyed a good scratch on one of the several scratching posts and trees scattered around the Rescue, as did the other cats.

"Instead of taking the time to show me places I should not scratch, and places where it was all right to scratch," Allie continued, *"and I'm quite quick, so I don't think it would have taken much time,"* she put in defensively, *"they chopped off the first phalanges on all of my paws, the tips, where the claws are,"* Allie finished.

Wyatt's face was horrified.

"The two leggeds seem to think that de-clawing is just pulling the claws out of the phalanges," Henry put in; he had overheard Wyatt's question, and joined

in the conversation. *"And that's bad enough. But it is much, much more than that."*

Allie was one of Henry's favorites, since the two of them had been at the Rescue the longest. Henry also thought that his all black silhouette paired with Allie's all white fur was a striking combination, and often wished she were at liberty in the Rescue more often than she was.

"Yes, it is much more," Allie agreed. *"My two leggeds were not unkind or cruel people, although they were unthinking,"* she declared. *"Perhaps dull witted as well, I am not sure. But clearly, they not only put themselves first, they did not have any idea of what cats—or any animal, really—are truly like,"* she explained. *"The idea that a cat has emotions, memories, and the right to a safe and healthy life was completely foreign to them,"* Allie concluded.

"And then they left you," Henry added in a sympathetic tone. He head-butted Allie, who responded in kind.

"Yes. They moved. I am not certain why they did not take me: they took the dog. He and I had worked out a companionable relationship, and missing him was almost as bad as being abandoned," Allie said. *"The two leggeds told me I'd be fine, because the house was on the street behind the diner, so there would be lots of mice, and scraps and such,"* Allie went on. *"It never occurred to them that I was an indoor cat and had been for more than ten years. I wasn't skilled at hunting, and the fact that I had no claws meant that it was very, very hard for me to catch anything."* She paused. *"It also didn't occur to them that the new owners of the*

house might not want me around: they didn't, and so I ended up living outside the diner. I did rely on scraps, but it wasn't the proper diet for a cat, and I was becoming ill. I probably would have died if Judy hadn't brought me here," she added in a quiet voice.

Chapter Twenty

Spring was taking a very long time coming that year, although since it was Wyatt's first spring, he didn't realize that. He would be a year old in June, and was filling out and becoming quite a good looking ginger cat.

He and another of the cats, Bella, often sat together and compared their markings. Bella was a silver tabby with swirls on her flanks. Wyatt also had swirls on his flanks, though because of the orange and cream combination, they were less pronounced than Bella's silver and black.

Wyatt thought Bella was a very pretty cat, too, even if her face was not as sweet as Shadow's or as appealing as Lemonie's or as delicately lovely as Renesme's. Like most of the cats at the Rescue, Bella seemed quite content with her situation, and grateful that she was somewhere warm and safe.

Wyatt, too, was thankful that he'd landed where he had. Even though it wasn't the same as a real forever home with a two legged to call his own, at least it was a forever home for him.

Then one rainy night Sara's truck pulled up in front of the Rescue. It had been raining for a day: solid, steady rain, and the creeks and rivers were rising in the small town where the Rescue was located. However, as the Rescue's building was on fairly high ground, it was not in danger. But the streets and storm drains and gutters were overflowing.

All the cats ran to the front windows when they heard Sara's truck engine. She lived just two doors down from the Rescue, so she usually walked over: what was she doing driving up?

"*Maybe she went shopping and has her truck filled with catnip and food!*" Melle chattered excitedly, and began chasing her tail.

"*Don't be silly, Melle,*" Oreo replied, but kindly: Melle's two leggeds had force fed her alcohol and kept her inebriated solely for their amusement. The Humane Officer had removed her from that place, and she'd been brought here to the Rescue. However, because of this, sometimes Melle's thought processes were, well, a bit simple, Oreo thought.

"*Maybe she brought litter,*" Renesme put in, ever practical. "*We can always use that, and it's heavy, so I'm sure Sara wouldn't want to walk over here with it,*"she finished logically.

But it was neither litter nor food nor catnip that Sara was bringing to the Rescue. To the cats' amazement, she withdrew a large plastic tub-like container from her truck, and then, carrying it carefully, brought it inside.

"*I smell cats,*" Wyatt whispered to Buffy, who nodded.

Sara brought the plastic tub quickly to the back room, the same room where Wyatt had been quarantined when he'd first arrived. She shut the door, though, so none of the cats could get in, telling them that she'd open the door in a few minutes.

The cats grouped together outside the door, listening intently to what was going on inside. Oreo, who was very clever and also very tall, stretched up against the door almost to the knob, and peered through the keyhole. Others went belly down, flat on the floor and tried to peek under the door but all they could see were Sara's shoes and the damp bottoms of her bluejeans.

"*She's opening the plastic tub,*" Oreo whispered to the others, who swiveled their ears and extended their whiskers to gather as much information as they could.

"*There's a lot of that silver tape on it,*" Oreo informed them. Then: "*Oh, my: it's a grey cat—and a kitten. No, two kittens,*" Oreo said in an amazed voice.

The cats murmured excitedly to each other.

"*What were they doing in a plastic bin?*" Renesme asked, shouldering her litter mate aside to try and look through the keyhole. But she was not quite tall enough, and resignedly dropped to all four paws and let her brother resume his watch post.

The cats listened avidly, and heard Sara say to the new cats that she couldn't imagine what the two legged who put them in the container had been thinking. There was a box of kibble and a towel in the container, but it had been taped shut, and if Oreo understood what Sara was saying correctly, some two legged had left the container on the side of the road.

"*Was that two legged insane?*" Renesme shrieked in outrage. "*Leaving a mother and two babies in a sealed container?*"

"*And by the side of the road?*" Wyatt queried, very confused. The way he'd been abandoned had been pretty bad, but at least he and poor Moo had been free to forage as they could, in an effort to survive. In a sealed container, these cats would have had no chance at all.

Then Oreo's whiskers stiffened in shock and he dropped to the floor. *"There's a big crack in the container's bottom,"* he informed the cats. *"If I understand what Sara is saying, the container had been left in the ditch at the side of the street, but because of the rain, that ditch had become full of water,"* he went on, wrinkling his nose when he said, 'water.'

"And with the crack in the container..." Renesme put in.

"They would have drowned," Wyatt finished in a dismayed whisper.

Oreo nodded. *"They do look pretty wet,"* he added, explaining that Sara was drying the mother cat and the two small kittens, whose eyes weren't even open yet, with a clean towel.

Next they heard sounds of a cage being prepared: newspaper, a litter box, towels and blankets, bowls, food, water. Then a few scrambling noises, and Sara's soothing voice.

Then she opened the door.

"Ok, guys, you can come in and see the new tenants," she announced with a smile. "But be good: they've had an awful time and they're tired," she urged them.

Chapter Twenty-one

The two tiny kittens and their mother were quite the objects of fascination for a couple of days. One of the kittens, sadly, died, and Sara took the tiny body away to give him a proper burial. She named him 'Lightning' because he had been with her so briefly.

The mother cat and the other kitten, however, thrived. Before long the mother cat, whom Sara had named Joan, was able to sit up and chat with the other cats as they came by her cage. She explained that she had originally been a farm cat, and had lost part of her tail in a discing machine when she'd only been a kitten. After it had healed, she related, she'd been given as a gift to a young family.

"But they were not very, well, very bright," Joan explained one afternoon when most of the residents of the Rescue were in the back room, visiting with her.

Judy had left and Sara wouldn't be by for a few hours, and it wasn't Paula's day to come, so everything was quiet.

"Of course, they let me roam outside, and of course I found a tomcat—or rather, he found me—and before we knew it, I had two kittens," Joan said. Her eyes were round and green and her grey fur was lightly tabby striped. Her face was round, too, and Wyatt thought she might have some Persian in her bloodlines, although far, far back.

"And they turned you out?" Renesme asked, sounding angry. She'd heard it so often, she was tired of hearing it, and it made her cross to think of this

defenseless mother cat and her tiny kittens being turned out into the street.

"Yes. But I think they thought they were providing for us," Joan replied, pondering. *"They put in food and a blanket, after all,"* she insisted.

Princess, who like the rest was very curious about the new arrivals, and had joined the group in the back room, was amazed that Joan was so forgiving. *"And then they sealed it shut so you couldn't get out,"* she said in a sarcastic tone. *"Really smart."*

Joan fluffed her fur, and licked one shoulder twice, nervously. *"Well, I told you, they weren't bright."*

Oreo snorted. *"That's an understatement."*

"Well, you're safe now," Shadow said, and Lemonie, next to her, nodded.

"Yes. You'll be taken care of, and fed, and kept warm and well," chimed in Maya.

Joan nodded, and her whiskers turned up. *"I am very grateful,"* she murmured, with a look at her sleeping kitten. *"We both are."*

Sara and Judy named the kitten Dazzle because from the moment she opened her eyes, she was like a little firecracker, always busy, always playing or climbing, and once she was big enough to be let out amongst the other cats, always going somewhere. Dazzle got into more tight places and high places and places where Judy and Sara and Paula and the other ladies who helped at the Rescue said in amazement, 'how did she get there?' than any other cat ever had.

But she was adorable, with very soft, thick fur. Everyone thought Dazzle would be adopted quickly, for from time to time Sara or Judy would bring two leggeds to the Rescue who had expressed interest in adopting one of the cats. However, this didn't happen, and Wyatt privately thought that perhaps Dazzle was meant to stay with her mother, Joan, who seemed to need the kitten rather more than the kitten needed her.

It was still quite cold by early April. Snow had fallen a day or so before, a couple of inches, just enough to make everything muddy and wet and gloomy looking again. Just like the two leggeds, cats also suffer from the shorter days and lack of sunlight during the long winter months. They need sunlight to manufacture vitamin D, as well, and when they don't get it, they can become lethargic and somewhat depressed.

That was why, as the days began to get longer and the sun's rays began to get stronger, the cats jockeyed for position in the big front windows of the Rescue. They managed to share the area pretty well, taking turns and lying perpendicularly to the window so that as many as possible could fit in the patches of weak sun.

Late one morning, Wyatt was taking advantage of the less crowded feeding stations to grab a few last mouthfuls of kibble, while most of the cats lounged in the sunny front room. Henry, Buffy, Brother and Bella were also with him in the kitchen when they heard the Rescue's door open.

It was Judy. What was she doing here, the cats wondered. She'd already been by to clean and feed and water, as usual.

Something made Wyatt look up from the bowl, and take a few steps towards the long hall that ran from the kitchen to the front room in the Rescue. He heard Judy saying something to another two legged— but it wasn't Sara or Paula or any of the other ladies who helped out. This two legged smelled different.

Suddenly, Wyatt remembered that odd dream he'd had weeks before, the one where a Tortoiseshell cat seemed to be trying to tell him something. She had seemed sad, that cat with the dark fur and the orange stripe on her nose. And she'd told him, in Wyatt's dream, to watch for a lady, a very special lady.

The dream had come to him so long ago, he'd still thought of himself as Squeaker: he'd been living rough on the porch of the house next door, and Moo had died not long before.

Now, Wyatt's head snapped up and he sniffed the new two legged's scent deeply. Then he came running down the hallway, his paws going as fast as he could make them, until he burst into the front room.

Judy was saying hello to the several cats who were gathering around her, asking if she were here to give them extra treats or something. And next to her, there stood a lady. She was smiling in that odd way that the two leggeds had, but Wyatt also saw that her cheeks were wet and her eyes were leaking.

He knew this meant the lady was very sad, so sad that her heart could not hold all her feelings and they spilled out through her eyes.

He walked purposefully up to her, through the other cats who were sniffing at her shoes and wondering who she was, and wound himself around her ankles, looking up at her the entire time.

"Oh, my goodness, who are you?" the lady asked, bending down and giving Wyatt a tentative stroke on his head.

"She's probably a new helper for Miss Judy, here at the Rescue," commented Shadow, who was hovering next to the lady's feet.

"She seems very nice: maybe she's here to adopt one of us!" Renesme wondered from a nearby perch.

"I've been waiting for you!" Wyatt said, leaning into the lady's hand to let her know he was happy to feel her touch. He also hoped she wouldn't start petting anyone else. He had a feeling about her: this was the lady that Tortoiseshell cat had told him about, he was sure of it.

Chapter Twenty-two

The lady scooped him up in her arms.

"Hello," she said, looking into his eyes.

He wanted to reach up and brush away her tears, but Wyatt settled for putting one paw on her shoulder and the other briefly on the side of her face.

"Well, aren't you friendly!" the lady said, and smiled a bit more.

"Oh, yes, he's very friendly," Judy agreed, "but not usually like that, I've never seen him do that," she added.

"What's his name?" the lady asked.

"We call him Wyatt," Judy replied.

"That's what they call me, but I don't think that's really my name," Wyatt said to the lady.

"Oh really?" the lady replied, looking him full in the face again.

Then she sat down in one of the chairs in the front room and Wyatt settled himself on her lap. Of course by now the other cats had finished greeting Judy and they wanted to see what the new two legged was all about. So they clustered around her ankles and a couple of the bolder ones jumped up on the chair next to the one she sat in and tried to climb over onto her lap.

But Wyatt stood his ground, and he told them to leave her alone.

"This lady is mine," he said to them. *"She is here for me."*

"Oh? And just how, pray tell, do you know that?" Maya asked in exasperation.

Wyatt looked determined. "*I had a dream, weeks and weeks ago, before I came here, even before I was rescued. In my dream, a cat I'd never seen before told me about a very special lady. She said she had to leave the lady, but that she was giving her to me.*"

Maya looked momentarily non plussed, then she snorted. "*Cats don't give two leggeds to other cats!*" she declared derisively. "*I've never heard anything so silly in my life!*"

Allie had arrived in the front room by this time, because Judy had brought her out to meet the new lady. From Judy's arms, Allie gave Maya a silencing glare, then she gazed at Wyatt, perched on the new lady's lap, and her whiskers tilted up.

"*It is true,*" Allie said softly. "*Sometimes cats who know their time is coming soon can see ahead, see things which may happen, and have a paw in directing the course of events,*" she explained.

Judy nuzzled her favorite cat lovingly.

Maya looked chastised.

"*I never understood that dream,*" Wyatt confessed. "*Was—was the Tortoiseshell cat ill?*" he asked Allie.

Beneath his paws, Wyatt felt the lady stiffen. It was almost as though she knew what he and Allie were saying.

Allie nodded. "*I believe so. But she knew your need, young Wyatt, and so she was able to come to you through the dream plane and tell you about this two legged.*" She paused, looking at the lady with great concentration. "*Her need is as great as yours, and that Tortoiseshell saw this, and has destined that you be together,"* Allie said.

Wyatt turned and looked up at the lady. *"Will you be my human?"* he ventured. It seemed wrong, somehow, to call her his Staff, and 'two legged' wasn't very respectful, really. He didn't want to jeopardize anything.

"I will," the lady said. "Even though I didn't come here to adopt a cat," she added.

Judy laughed.

"But—will you be my cat?" the lady asked Wyatt then, solemnly. "I'll have to call you something else," she added, more to herself than to him.

"I will," he said happily, and rubbed the sides of his face on her hands, and purred.

The lady continued to stroke him, and Judy brought Allie back to her room, and then busied herself with the chores that always were waiting for anyone who helped out at the Rescue.

The other cats, understanding that the lady would never be theirs, but belonged now to Wyatt, drew back and returned to their sunbathing or grooming or sleeping.

"I think—I think I'd like to call you Raphael," the lady said, having thought for a few minutes as she continued to stroke Wyatt, who remained on her lap. "That's an Angel's name, the Angel of Healing," she told him, and her voice began to quiver again. "I would like that to be your name, because I think you will heal my heart," she explained, and her eyes began to leak again.

"That's a wonderful name! I like it. I think it fits me. I am happy to be called Raphael," Raphael

said, pushing his head into her hands to show her how glad he was.

A couple of salty drops from the lady's eyes fell on Raphael's fur, but he didn't mind.

"You see, I had a cat, a wonderful cat, named Nike," the lady went on, speaking now in a very low voice that only Raphael could hear. "She was with me for thirteen years. But she was quite old, and became ill, and she died, just last week," the lady said. "And today, something told me I should find my friend Judy and come visit the cats at her Rescue," she went on. "Even though I didn't intend to adopt anyone..."

Raphael kept purring, and looking at the lady.

"Well, then, I guess it's settled—Raphael," the lady said, and she smiled, and dried her tears with the hand that wasn't stroking Raphael.

Judy came back into the front room at this point and grinned. "I think you found your next cat," she commented.

The lady laughed. "Yes. Or he found me," she amended. "I'll have to go get a few things," she went on, speaking to Judy, but of course Raphael was listening intently. "I threw away all of Nike's toys and her cat bed and such, I couldn't bear to look at them," the lady said sadly.

Thinking her eyes might start to leak again, Raphael reached a paw up to her face and said, *"but you have me now, don't cry."*

The lady smiled at him. "I know I have you now, Raphael," she said.

She understood me! Raphael thought in surprise. She really, really knew what I'd said! Not like Laura, who had done a good job of guessing what he or Tuesday had told her: this lady appeared to really comprehend his squeaky meows!

"But I still get sad when I think of Nike," she finished.

"*Of course, I understand*," Raphael said.

"Anyway," the lady looked up at Judy again. "Give me a few days to get everything—I'll have to get new insurance and get his tags made, and find a nice leather collar to put them on," she said.

"*A collar?*" Raphael asked, excited.

"Yes, a collar—I'll get a handsome one, handsome, just like you," she told him.

Raphael remembered Tuesday's words: '*a collar means I belong to someone.*' He cuddled closer to the lady, and put his face in her hands as she continued to stroke him.

A collar. A collar! That meant he belonged to this lady now. That he would have a forever home with her for as long as he lived. That she would watch out for him, and keep him safe and healthy, and buy him treats and toys, and play with him, and that they would always be together.

Raphael heard Judy say that there was no rush, that the lady could just let her know when she wanted to come and pick him up.

And then finally, the lady said she had to leave, but that she would be back the next day to visit, and that in just a few days, Raphael would be coming home with her. Then, after a few more good byes, she put Raphael gently on the floor, and stood, and followed Judy out of the Rescue.

Chapter Twenty-three

Raphael did go home with the lady, whom he very soon came to call 'Mum.' He was sad to leave his friends at the Rescue, but excited to think he would have his very own forever home now.

The lady had promised to come visit the cats at the Rescue often and let them know how Raphael was doing.

"*We'll be able to smell you on her,*" Oreo had assured Raphael on his last night with them all. "So we'll know how you are."

They had all gathered in the big front room where there were many pillows and cat beds, a cat tree and other spots to lounge and have a conversation. Night lights glowed and a shaft of silver from a streetlight outside illuminated the room, too.

Raphael was once again sharing a big squishy soft bed with Oreo, and it seemed everyone else was arranged in a semi circle around them. He could even see Brother and the more timid cats on the edges of the group: they'd all come together to say goodbye and wish him well.

"*I'll miss you,*" Raphael said honestly to the cats.

"*We will miss you, too, but you will have a great life with that lady,*" Oreo assured him. "*As much as we are happy for company sometimes, and litter mates usually get on better together than random pairings,*" he added with an admonishing look at his sister, Renesme, who often pranked him, "*most of the time we are delighted to be alone. Being an only cat in a good forever home is about the best life a cat can have.*"

Raphael sighed happily. "*The lady did mention something I am not quite sure I understand,*" he went on. "*She said there is something at her house called a 'screened porch' that I will be able to go in and enjoy. Now, I know what a porch is, but what is a screen?*" he asked.

"*Oh, a screened porch!*" Princess piped up from the side of the semi circle where she was situated on a pillow. "*I know what those are. Screen is a metal mesh that lets you see outside, and lets breezes and smells in, but keeps bugs and other animals and things out. You're safe, but it's almost like being outside.*"

"*Like having a really big windowsill,*" Snaps put in helpfully.

Raphael thought a moment. He didn't remember the windows in Jenna's room ever being open, so he had no experience with screens. But what Princess had described sounded amazing.

"*Wow,*" he breathed.

"*You're one lucky kitty!*" Henry pronounced. He had to try very hard to keep the resentment from his voice. Of course, he was happy for his pal, but he couldn't help wishing the lady with the screened porch had picked him instead.

Renesme nodded. "*You are. And I kinda think that lady is pretty special,*" she said, sounding just a little envious. "*She could have adopted me, too,*" she murmured petulantly. "*Two aren't any more trouble than one...*"

But her brother shook his head.

"No: Raphael was meant for her. And she for him," Oreo said. "Remember what the cat in Raphael's dream said, and what our Allie counseled," he added gravely.

Raphael had finally told all the cats at the Rescue about his dream. He'd given as much detail as he could remember, much more than the sketchy outline he'd given Maya. And even she, who had ridiculed him for believing his dream, had to admit that the fit between him and the lady seemed to be right.

"Well, Raphael, maybe we can all hope to have a dream like yours," Maya said now, apologetically. "I would love to find a forever home," she repeated, and looked sad.

"I hope you do, Maya," Raphael replied. He looked around at all of them: Oreo, Renesme, Buffy, Shadow, Maya, Melle, Henry, Lemonie, Hootie, Princess, Brother, Bella, Joan, Dazzle, Allie, Snaps, and even MamaKitty and her offspring. "I hope you all find forever homes."

You are Safe, You are Home, You are Loved

I'd been lost for quite some time,
All alone, no one to call mine.
Then one night I had a dream:
'You will meet a woman,
But she is not as she seems.
Behind her brave and smiling face,
Her heart is torn in two.
I had to leave her, though I did not wish it,
But there was nothing I could do.'
I blinked my little kitten eyes,
'But how can I help her?
I am an abandoned kitten,
With unkempt, scraggly fur!?'
The wise voice in my dream answered
As though from a far place:
'You will know her when you meet her,
You will see your love in her face.'
I did not understand,
And I had important things to do:
Surviving, finding food each day,
And a place to to curl up, too.
Then one day, I was rescued:
Fed and cleaned and taken care,
I would survive in this new haven,
But there were lots of kitties there.
I did not think about the dream
I'd had some weeks before;
I ate and slept and played and wondered,
If I would ever know any more.
I had heard tales of 'home' and 'love'
And though surely I was now safe,
I knew this wasn't what the other cats meant
When they spoke of their own 'family' and 'place.'
Then one day the Rescue door opened,
And something made me run ahead.

I saw a woman, smiling,
And I remembered what my dream voice had said!
The lady's smile was shaky,
And her eyes were wet with tears.
So I wound myself around her ankles
And miaowed that I would end her fears.
'I have been waiting for you,'
I told her when she sat.
She scooped me up into her lap,
And whispered, 'will you be my cat?'
She calls me Raphael, the Angel with healing
in his wings.
She says I have healed her heart, and taken away
death's sting.
I don't know how I did that: I am only
a little orange cat.
She calls me her classic red tabby,
And I am okay with that.
I have a home of my own now, a Family,
and dozens of toys.
I start each day with a full food bowl
and end it by Mum's side.
I think I must be lucky, and I thank
the dream cat who gave
Me her Mum when she had to leave her,
the lady both sad and brave.
I wish all kitties could have what I've found:
As my Mum tells me, and I think it is true,
When the stars twinkle down
and we drift off to sleep,
'You are safe, you are home, you are loved.'

--Raphael Charlemagne Jefferson Courville 6/2014

From Raphael:

Dear Reader:
Thank you for reading my story. I hope you enjoyed it and I hope it made you think about the welfare of animals in today's world.
Most of the cats at the Cat Ladies' Rescue mentioned in my story are available for adoption, and there are many more now, too. If you're interested in opening your home to one or more of my pals, please email my Mum. Her email is at the beginning of this book on the 'About the Author' page.

Love,
Raphael